Jerzy Kosinski's
STEPS

"Some of the episodes suggest Babel, some a darker Dinesen, some de Maupassant.... Kosinski makes his book so scorchingly personal that it is unique. Kosinski's style, simple and precise, not overtly emotional, is a style made of small, deceptively plain, exploding capsules. A very large achievement."
— Stanley Kaufmann, *New Republic*

"Violent sexual experiences told with shocking, unemotional vividness."
— *Harper's*

"One of the finest books of the year... Kosinski is almost alone among writers of his generation in the severity of his challenge to man's capacity for self-knowledge — for as we hold the mirror to Medusa's face, we find that the image is our own."
— *Playboy*

JERZY KOSINSKI
STEPS

Vintage Contemporaries

Vintage Books
A Division of Random House
New York

First Vintage Contemporaries Edition, January 1988

Library of Congress Cataloging-in-Publication Data
Kosinski, Jerzy N., 1933–
Steps.
(Vintage contemporaries)
I. Title.
PS3561.O8S7 1988   813'.54   87-40279
ISBN 0-394-75716-5 (pbk.)

Author photo by Scientia Factum

Manufactured in the United States of America

10   9   8   7   6   5   4   3   2   1

TO MY FATHER, *a mild man*

For the uncontrolled there is no wisdom, nor for the uncontrolled is there the power of concentration; and for him without concentration there is no peace. And for the unpeaceful, how can there be happiness?

THE BHAGAVADGĪTĀ

S T E P S

I WAS TRAVELING farther south. The villages were small and poor; each time I stopped in one, a crowd gathered around my car and the children followed my every move.

I decided to spend a couple of days in a bare whitewashed village to rest and have my clothes washed and mended. The woman who undertook the job for me explained that she could get it done promptly and efficiently because she employed a helper—a young orphan girl who had to support herself. She pointed to a girl star-ing at us from a window.

When I returned to collect my laundry the next day, I met the girl in the front room. She only occasionally lifted up her eyes to me. Whenever our eyes met, she would attempt to conceal her interest in me by bending her head lower and lower over her sewing.

While I was transferring some of my documents to the pocket of my freshly pressed jacket, I noticed the curiosity with which she glanced at the plastic credit cards I had placed momentarily on the table. I asked her if she knew what they were; she replied that she had never seen anything like them before. I told her that with any one of these cards one could buy furniture, bed linen, kitchenware, food, clothing, stockings, shoes, handbags, perfumes, or almost anything else one wanted without paying any money.

Nonchalantly I continued explaining to her that I could also use my cards in the most expensive stores in the nearby town, that just to show them would be enough to have food served to me in any restaurant, that I could stay in the best hotels, and that I could do all this for myself as well as for anyone else I chose. I added that because I liked her and thought she looked nice, and because I sensed that she was being mistreated by her employer, I would like to take her away with me. If she wished, she could stay with me as long as she liked.

Still without looking at me she asked, as if wanting to be reassured, whether she would need to have any money. Again I told her that neither she nor I would need any money provided we had the cards with us and wanted to use them. I promised her that the two of us would travel to different cities and even countries; she wouldn't have to work or do anything other than take care of herself, I would buy her anything she'd want, she could wear beautiful clothes and look lovely for me and change her hair styles or even the color of her hair as often as she wished. For this to come about, I said, all she had to do was to leave her house late that night without a word to anyone and meet me at the road sign on the outskirts of the village. Upon reaching the big town, I assured her, a letter would be sent to her employer explaining that like so many girls before her, she had left home in order to find a job in the big city. Finally I told her I would be waiting for her that night, and I very much hoped she would come.

The credit cards lay on the table. She got up and stared at them with reverence in which disbelief mingled; she stretched her right hand forward as if to touch them, but quickly withdrew it. I picked up a card and handed it to her. She held it gingerly between her fingers like a sacramental wafer, raising it to the light to inspect the numbers and letters printed on it.

That evening I parked my car in some bushes several yards from the road sign. Before it grew completely dark, many carts passed on their way from the market to the village, but no one noticed me.

Suddenly the girl appeared from behind me, short of breath and frightened, clutching a bundle of her belongings. I opened the car door, and without a word, beckoned her into the rear seat. I started the engine promptly, and only after we had left the village did I slow down and tell her that she was now free and that her days of poverty were over. She sat very quietly for a while and then, uncertain, asked me if I still had my cards. I removed them from my pocket and handed them to her. A few minutes later I could no longer see her head in the rear-view mirror: she had fallen asleep.

We arrived in the city late the next morning. She awoke and glued her face to the window, watching the traffic. Suddenly she touched my arm, pointing to the large department store we were passing. She would like to find out, she said, whether it was true that my cards exercised more power than money did. I parked the car.

Inside the store she clung to my arm, and I felt the palm of her hand damp from excitement. She had never been in the city before, she confessed, nor even in a small town, and she couldn't believe so many people could gather in one place and yet leave so many things still to be bought. She pointed at dresses she liked, and she agreed to my few suggestions of the things that would be most becoming for her. Assisted by two shop-girls who looked at my companion with obvious envy, we selected several pairs of shoes, gloves, stockings, some underwear, a number of dresses and handbags, and a coat.

Now she was even more frightened. When I asked her whether she was afraid that my cards could not pay for all that we had chosen, she tried to deny her fear at first, then finally admitted it. Why, she asked me, would so many people in her village labor all their lives to earn enough money to pay for all we had bought, when I, who was not a famous soccer player or movie star, not even a prelate, seemed to have no need of any money at all to acquire everything I wanted.

When all our purchases were packed, I handed the cashier one of the cards; she thanked me politely, disappeared for a moment, and then came back and returned the card with the bill of sale. My friend stood behind me, eager to grab the box but still afraid to do so.

We left the store. When we got into the car, the girl opened the package and looked over her things, touching them, sniffing them, touching them again, closing and opening the box. As I drove off, she began to try on the shoes and gloves. We pulled up in front of a small hotel and went inside. Disregarding the hotel clerk's knowing glance, I requested a suite of adjoining rooms. My luggage was carried upstairs, but the girl insisted on carrying the box herself, as though fearing it might be taken from her.

In the suite, she went to her room to change and returned dressed in a new gown. She paraded in front of me, moving awkwardly in her new high-heeled shoes, looking at herself in the mirror, returning to her room again and again to try the other outfits.

The remaining packages containing various articles of underwear were delivered by the store in the late afternoon. By then the girl was slightly giddy from the wine we had drunk at lunch, and now, as if trying to impress me with her newly acquired worldliness she must have learned from film and glamour magazines, she stood before me, her hands on her hips, her tongue moistening her lips, and her unsteady gaze seeking out my own.

17

There were several of us, all archeological assistants, working on one of the islands with a professor who for years had been excavating remnants of an ancient civilization that had flourished fifteen centuries before our era.

It was an advanced civilization, the professor claimed, but at some point a massive catastrophe had wiped it out. He had challenged the prevailing theory that a disastrous earthquake, followed by a tidal wave, had struck the island. We were collecting fragments of pottery, sifting through ashes for the remains of artifacts, and unearthing building materials, all of which the professor catalogued as evidence to support his as yet unpublished work.

After a month I decided to leave the excavations and visit a neighboring island. In my haste to catch the ferry I left without my paycheck, but I obtained the promise that it would be forwarded on the next mail skiff. I could live for one day on the money I had with me.

After arriving I spent the entire day sightseeing. The island was dominated by a dormant volcano, its broad slopes covered with porous lava rock, weathered to form a poor but arable soil.

I walked down to the harbor; an hour before sunset, when the air was cooling, the fishing boats put out for the night. I watched them slide over the calm, almost waveless water until their long, low forms vanished from sight. The islands suddenly lost the light reflected from their rocky spines and grew stark and black. And then, as though drawn silently beneath the surface, they disappeared one by one.

On the morning of the second day I went down to the quay to meet the mail skiff. To my consternation my paycheck had not arrived. I stood on the dock, wondering how I was going to live and whether I would even be able to leave the island. A few fishermen sat by their nets, watching me; they sensed that something was wrong. Three of them approached and spoke to me. Not understanding, I replied in the two languages I knew: their faces became sullen and hostile, and they abruptly turned away. That evening I took my sleeping bag down to the beach and slept on the sand.

In the morning I spent the last of my money on a cup of coffee. After strolling up the winding streets behind the port, I walked through the scrubby fields to the nearest village. The villagers sat in the shade, covertly watching me. Hungry and thirsty, I returned to the beach again, walking beneath a blazing sun. I had nothing to barter for food or money: no watch, no fountain pen, no cuff links, no camera, no wallet. At noon, when the sun stood high and the villagers sheltered in their cottages, I went to the police station. I found the island's solitary policeman dozing by the telephone. I woke him, but he seemed reluctant to understand even my simplest gesture. I pointed to his phone, pulling out my empty pockets; I made signs and drew pictures, even miming thirst and hunger. All this had no effect: the policeman showed neither interest nor understanding, and the phone remained locked. It was the only one on the island; the guidebook I had read had even bothered to note the fact.

In the afternoon I strolled around the village, smiling at the inhabitants, hoping to be offered a drink or to be invited to a meal. No one returned my greeting; the villagers turned away and the storekeepers simply ignored me. The church was on the largest island of the group and I had no means of getting there to ask for food and shelter. I returned to the beach as if expecting help to rise up from the sea. I was famished and exhausted. The sun had brought on a pounding headache, I felt waves of vertigo. Unexpectedly I caught the sound of people talking in an alien language. Turning, I saw two women sitting close to the water. Folds of gray, heavily veined fat hung from their thighs and upper arms; their full, pendulous breasts were squashed in outsize brassieres.

They sunbathed sprawling on their beach towels surrounded by picnic equipment: food baskets, thermos flasks, parasols, and nets full of fruit. A pile of books, heaped up alongside, conspicuously displayed library numbers. They were evidently tourists staying with a local family. I approached them slowly but directly, anxious not to alarm them. They stopped talking, and I greeted them smilingly, using my languages in turn. They replied in another one. We had no common language, but I was very conscious of the proximity of food. I sat down beside them as though I had understood I had been invited. When they began to eat I eyed the food;

they either did not notice this or ignored my intense stare. After a few minutes the woman I judged to be the older offered me an apple. I ate it slowly, trying to conceal my hunger and hoping for something more solid. They watched me intently.

It was hot on the beach and I dozed off. But I woke when the two women pulled themselves to their feet, their shoulders and back red from the sun. Rivulets of perspiration streaked the sand that clung to their flabby thighs, the fat slid over their hips as they braced themselves to stoop and collect their belongings. I helped them. With flirtatious nods they set off along the inner rim of the beach; I followed.

We reached the house they occupied. On entering I was hit by another wave of vertigo; I stumbled on a step and collapsed. Laughing and chattering, the women undressed me and maneuvered me onto a large, low bed. Still dazed, I pointed to my stomach. There was no delay: they rushed to bring me meat, fruit, and milk. Before I could finish the meal, they had drawn the curtains and torn off their bathing suits. Naked, they fell upon me. I was buried beneath their heavy bellies and broad backs; my arms were pinioned; my body was manipulated, squeezed, pressed, and thumped.

I was at the dock at dawn. The mail skiff came in, but there was neither a check nor a letter for me. I stood there watching the boat recede into the hot sun that dissolved the morning mist, revealing one by one the distant islands.

●

I was employed as a skiing instructor and lived in a mountain resort where tubercular patients were sent for care. I occupied an apartment from which I could see the sanatorium and distinguish the pale faces of the new arrivals from the tanned faces of the long-term patients who sunned themselves on the terraces.

At the end of each afternoon my tired skiers would return to their hostels, and I to my solitary dinner. I spent most of my time alone. After supper the muffled sounds of the gong from the sanatorium would announce the night routine, and a few minutes later the lights would be extinguished, as if snatched from one window after the next.

A dog howled from a hut far up on the slopes. Somewhere a door clanged shut. Then I caught sight of human figures struggling through the deep snow of a nearby field: the skiing instructors from neighboring hostels were moving in stealthily for their nocturnal encounters. From the massive blackness surrounding the sanatorium several figures hurried toward the men waiting below: female patients were sneaking out to meet their lovers. The silhouettes touched and merged as if they were the fragments of a shadow being mended. Each couple left separately. In the moonlight they looked like dwarfed mountain pines which had stepped down from the slopes to venture among the windless fields. Soon they were all gone.

In the weeks that followed I became aware that some of the stronger patients were permitted to spend part of each day outdoors. They met at the café at the foot of the slopes, and many of them formed alliances with the tourists and members of the staff. Quite often, from the shelter provided by a copse of firs, I would watch them pairing off, noticing every now and then a change in partners and committing to memory those who were especially sought after and those who were neglected. Then, as the last vestiges of light faded and it suddenly grew chilly even in my sheltered lookout, I would turn and make my way back to my lodgings.

There was one woman I observed in particular. She had not been a serious case, and it was said that her recovery was excellent: she was to be discharged at the end of the month. Two men were competing for her —a young skiing instructor from a neighboring hotel, and a tourist who had often spoken of staying at the resort until the woman was discharged.

The woman divided her attention equally between the two men. Every afternoon the tourist hurried over from his hotel, while the instructor skied in after dismissing his class. The woman would sit in the café at the foot of the slopes. She could watch both her suitors making their various approaches.

The instructor played upon his skills, skiing over at the highest possible speed and, when it seemed almost too late, turning violently away from the terrace rail and skidding in a spray of snow alongside the woman's table. His rival, only a fair skier, would wander around at the foot of the slopes, forcing the instructor to slow up or pull away and usually disrupting the speed and deftness of his descent.

One afternoon I arrived at the café before the skiing classes were over. The tourist was already there, apparently unwilling to continue his clumsy maneuvers on the slopes. The instructor had taken his pupils to the nursery slopes above and to one side of the café. As the sun began to sink, he dismissed the class, but did not push off from the top of the slope as was his habit when skiing down to the café. Instead, he began moving up along a snow-covered ridge. The ridge was always marked with danger flags, and was forbidden to all but the national medalists. People left their tables and crowded against the terrace rail to watch his slow ascent. The woman jumped up and ran out of the restaurant to the foot of the slope to wait for him. The tourist followed.

The instructor launched himself, at first swooping down in long, graceful curves, avoiding the shoulders of raw rock that broke through the snow and gave the trail its reputation for danger. He picked up speed continuously, skiing with the suppleness and precision of a master. I wondered whether he would stop at the post that marked the foot of the trail or end with a spectacular turn at the feet of the girl. Everyone was silent. The long, almost horizontal rays of the sun caught the woman and the tourist as they stood at the foot of the run.

The instructor swung into the last hundred yards, moving fast and straight. The girl shook off the tourist's hand, which was resting on hers, and stepped forward, raising her arms and calling out the instructor's name. The tourist lurched after her, grabbing her by the shoulder. In a second the instructor soared into the end of the run and gathered himself up as he might at the start of a jump, but instead of throwing himself forward and up, he seemed to thrust to the left in an unnaturally abrupt twist. No longer able either to turn or slow down, his skis lifted and he soared on, with the entire force and impetus that the long run had built up within him crashing suddenly with his shoulder into the man's unprotected chest. Both bodies slid for some distance down the slope, finally coming to rest at the edge of the terrace. The crowd rushed to them; blood dripped from the tourist's mouth and he was carried unconscious into the café. The instructor sat on the terrace steps for a few minutes, with his head in his hands, while the woman loosened his parka. Then the ambulance drove up, and the tourist, still unconscious, was strapped onto the stretcher. As the bearers picked him up I glanced toward the terrace steps. The instructor and the woman were no longer in sight.

I did not see the instructor again until much later. Then I saw him one evening with a woman.

They were sheltered in a recess in the stonework of the hotel wall. All around a storm raged, and the snow in the fields churned like water in a frenzied bay. Foaming drifts roared and formed, only to collapse like mounds of goose feathers into unfathomable clefts. Leaning against the wall and touched occasionally by the wavering light of the lantern that dangled above a foot-path, the man stood below the woman and drew her close to him. The woman bent toward him, clinging to his chest, yielding and tender. Her arms clasped his shoulders. The whirlwind tugged at her coat, pulling it open. For a moment they looked as if they had both suddenly grown wings which would carry them away from that niche, from those powdery fields and out of my sight. I made up my mind.

The next afternoon I found a pretext to visit the sanatorium. Patients in brightly patterned pullovers and tight pants strolled about the corridors. Others slept huddled in blankets. Filmy shadows cut across the deserted deck chairs on the sunny terrace, and the canvas snapped in the sharp breezes that scattered down from the peaks.

I saw a woman reclining in a chair. Her shawl, casually thrown around her shoulders, exposed her long, suntanned neck. As I lingered, gazing, she glanced at me thoughtfully, and then smiled. My shadow fell across her when I introduced myself.

The visiting rules were very strict, and I was permitted to spend only two hours a day in her room. I couldn't get too close to her: she would not let me. She was very ill and coughed continually. Often she brought up blood. She shivered, became feverish; her cheeks flushed. Her hands and feet would sweat.

During one of my visits she asked me to make love to her. I locked the door. After I had undressed she told me to look into the large mirror in the corner of the room. I saw her in the mirror and our eyes met. Then she got up from the bed, took off her robe, and stepped over to the mirror. She stood very close to it, touching my reflection with one hand and pressing her body with the other. I could see her breasts and her flanks. She waited for me while I concentrated more and more on the thought that it was I who stood there within the mirror and that it was my flesh her hands and lips were touching.

But in a low yet urgent voice, she would stop me whenever I took a step toward her. We would make love again: she standing as before in front of the mirror, and I, a pace away, my sight riveted upon her.

Her life was measured and constantly checked by various instruments, recorded on negatives, charted and filed away by a succession of doctors and nurses, reinforced by needles piercing her chest and veins, breathed in from oxygen bottles and breathed out into tubes. My brief visits were interrupted more and more frequently by the intrusion of doctors, nurses, or attendants who came to change the oxygen cylinders or give new medicines.

One day an older nun stopped me in the corridor. She asked me whether I knew what I was doing, and when I said I didn't understand, she said the staff had a name for people like myself: *hyaenidae*. As I still failed to understand, she said: hyenas. Men of my kind, she said, lurked around bodies that were dying; each time I fed upon the woman, I hastened her death.

As time went on her condition visibly deteriorated. I sat in her room, staring at her pale face lit only by an occasional flush. The hands on the bedspread were thin, with a delicate network of bluish veins. Her frail

shoulders heaving with every breath, she surrepti
wiped off the perspiration which rose steadily on he
head. I sat quietly and stared at the mirror whil
slept; it reflected the cold, white rectangles of the
and ceiling.

The nuns glided silently in and out of the
room, but I succeeded in never meeting their eyes. They
bent over the patient, wiping her forehead, moistening
her lips with wads of cotton, whispering some secret language into her ears. Their clumsy dresses flapped like the
wings of restless birds.

I would step out onto the terrace, quickly closing the door behind me. The wind was ceaselessly driving
the snow over the crusted fields, filling the deep foot-
prints and diagonal tracks left from the previous day. I
held the soft plump cushion of fresh snow from the
frozen railings. For a moment it shimmered in my warm
palm before turning into dripping slush.

More and more often I was denied access to
her room, and I spent those hours alone in my apartment. Later, before going to sleep, I would pull out from
the desk drawer several albums filled with my photographs of her, carefully enlarged and painstakingly pasted
onto stiff cardboard. I would place these enlargements
in a corner of my bedroom and sit in front of them, recalling the events of the hospital room and the images
within the mirror. In some of the photographs she was
naked; now I had them before me, for myself alone. I
looked at these pictures as if they were mirrors in which
I could see at any moment my own face floating ghost-
like on her flesh.

Then I would step out on my balcony. Around the sanatorium the lights from the windows touched the snow, which no longer seemed fresh. I would gaze at the faint lights until they began to disappear. From beyond the breadth and width of the valleys and hills, streaked by wooded slopes, the moonlight lit up frozen peaks and streams of vaporous clouds being lured from the shadows of narrow defiles.

A door clanged shut; a car horn sounded in the distance. Suddenly figures appeared between the snow-drifts. They scrambled through the fields toward the sanatorium, now and then lost, as if straining against the stifling dust storm of a drought-stricken plain.

•

I got off the train at a small station. As it pulled out I was the only one eating in the station restaurant. I stopped the waiter and asked if there was anything of interest happening locally. He looked at me and said there was to be a private show that afternoon in a nearby village.

He intimated that the performance would be rather unusual and that if I were willing to pay the price, he could arrange for me to see it. I agreed, and we left the station. Half an hour later we reached a paddock with a large carriage house at one end. About fifty middle-aged peasants had gathered under the trees near the building, where they sauntered about, smoking and jesting.

A man dressed in city clothes came out of the carriage house and began collecting money from all of us. The price represented about two weeks of a peasant's income, yet they all seemed willing to pay.

Then the organizer disappeared into the house, and we formed a circle screened by the trees. The peasants waited, whispering and laughing. A few minutes passed; the door of the carriage house opened and four women in colorful dresses walked into the circle. The organizer followed behind them leading a large animal. The peasants suddenly stopped talking. The women now stood next to each other, turning around so the men could see them, while the organizer paraded the animal.

The women seemed to represent particular types: one was very tall and powerfully built, another was a slender, fragile young girl whose appearance suggested she came from the city. All the women wore heavy make-up and tight short-skirted dresses. The peasants began discussing the women aloud, arguing excitedly. After a few minutes the organizer asked for quiet and explained that a vote would be taken to determine which woman would be chosen. As the women strolled around the arena, stretching, bending, and caressing their bodies, the crowd grew even more animated. The organizer called on them to vote for each woman in turn.

From the final count it became clear that the majority had elected the young girl. The three other women joined the audience, giggling and whispering with the men.

The chosen girl now sat alone in the circle. I scrutinized the men's faces; they seemed curious whether the girl would prove too frail and weak to survive her ordeal.

The organizer led the animal into the center of the arena, prodding its slack parts with a stick. Two peasants ran up and grabbed at the animal to keep it still. The girl then stepped forward and began playing with the creature, embracing and hugging it, fondling its genitals. She slowly began to undress. The animal was now aroused and restless. It seemed inconceivable that the girl could accommodate it.

The men became frantic, urging her to undress completely and couple with the animal. The organizer tied several ribbons on the animal's organ, each colored bow an inch apart. The girl approached the animal, rubbing oil into her thighs and abdomen and coaxing the animal to lick her body. Then, to shouts of encouragement, she lay down beneath the animal, clasping it with her legs. Raising up her belly and thrusting it forward, she forced an insertion up to the first bow. The organizer took control again, asking the audience to pay extra for each additional inch of the animal's involvement. The price was raised for each consecutive bow removed. The peasants, still refusing to believe that the girl could survive her violation, eagerly paid again and again. Finally the girl began to scream. But I was not sure if she was actually suffering or was only playing up to the audience.

•

I went to the zoo to see an octopus I had read about. It was housed in an aquarium and fed on live crabs, fish, mussels—and on itself. It nibbled at its own tentacles, consuming them one after another.

Obviously the octopus was slowly killing itself. One attendant explained that in the part of the world where it had been caught, an octopus was believed to be a god of war, prophesying defeat when it looked landward and victory when it loooked seaward; this particular specimen, the natives had claimed, had only looked landward when captured. A man jokingly remarked that by eating itself it was presumably acknowledging its own defeat.

Each time the octopus bit into itself, some of the spectators shuddered as if they felt it eating their own flesh. Others were impassive. Just as I was about to leave, I noticed a young woman staring at the octopus without any apparent reaction, her lips relaxed. There was a serenity about her that went beyond unconcern.

I approached and engaged her in conversation. She turned out to be the wife of a well-known public official whose family lived in the city. Before the afternoon was over she invited me to a dinner party she was giving at her home.

It was an imposing household, and the dinner party flawless. The hostess behaved very naturally, attending equally to her family and guests, and yet somehow she seemed quite remote. I thought she had glanced at me with a suggestion of intimate interest, and I wanted proof of this. I planned to leave the city the next day. This would be my only opportunity.

She had just turned away from a departing couple, and stood, drink in hand, near one of the library bookcases. With an assumed casualness I told her I wished to see her alone, for I couldn't free myself from the images she excited in me.

I proposed a meeting. I suggested the capital of the neighboring country to which I was going the next day. She was just about to answer when several guests approached us. She turned toward them but first handed me her glass as though it had been mine, quietly stating the name of the hotel where she would join me.

During the next few days I thought of her constantly, recalling every moment I had spent near her. I speculated about the other men at the party, about which of them might have been her lovers, and about various situations in which she had made love. The more I meditated about her, the more concerned I became about our first encounter.

. . . We were both naked. There was nothing I wanted so much as to be at ease with her. But the very thought of what she might expect from me made me less aroused. It was almost as though my thinking had to subside before my body could perform.

Yet I could not conceal my inadequacy, for in her mind, it seemed, my desire was reflected only in one part of me, a part suddenly grown very small. She blamed herself for what she insisted was her lack of finesse in gratifying me. She became increasingly frustrated and upset. I dressed and left her, walking the streets and trying to understand what had happened. I tried to decide how, in the future, I would explain my predicament to her; I was afraid she might reject any discussion as merely an excuse for a second futile attempt at physical intimacy.

On the street I approached a woman: her face was thickly painted and the shape of her figure lost in an ill-fitting dress. After some talk, she agreed to accompany me.

In the room she helped me to undress and then, still clothed herself, she began to caress me. There was a familiarity to her touch, as though her hands were guided over my skin by the current she felt pulsing underneath it; had I desired to use my own hands on my body, I would have guided them along the same path.

I looked again at her dress and suddenly realized my partner was a man. My mood altered abruptly. I felt the longing for pleasure and abandonment inside me, but I also sensed that I had been accepted too readily, that everything had suddenly become very predictable. All we could do was to exist for each other solely as a reminder of the self.

•

When I was in the army, many of the soldiers used to play a game in which about twenty or twenty-five men would sit around a table, each of them with a long string tied to his organ. The players were known as the "Knights of the Round Table." One man, whom we called King Arthur, held in his hand all the ends of the strings without knowing who was at the other end of each.

At intervals King Arthur would select a string and pull it, inch by inch, over the notched markings on the table top. The soldiers scanned each other's faces, aware that one of them was suffering. The victim would do all he could to conceal his pain and maintain his normal posture. It was said that the few men who were circumcised could not play the game as well as those who were not circumcised, whose shaft was protected by a foreskin. Bets would be made to see how many notches the string would pass over before the torture victim would cry out. Some soldiers ruined themselves for life by sitting out the game just to win the prize money.

I remember the occasion when the soldiers discovered that King Arthur had conspired with one of the men by tying the string around his leg. Naturally, this soldier was able to endure more pain than the others, and thus King Arthur and he succeeded in pocketing large sums of money. The cheated knights secretly selected the punishment they thought fitting. The guilty men were grabbed from behind, blindfolded, and taken into the forest. There they were stripped and tied to trees. The knights, one after another, slowly crushed each of the victim's parts between two rocks until the flesh became an unrecognizable pulp.

/ 25

•

Later, in the army, there was a group of twelve of us, and at night in our tent we used to talk about women. One of the men griped that he could never really do all he wanted to do—or at least, never for long enough—while making love to his woman. Some of the others seemed to have similar problems. I wasn't sure I understood, but it struck me that they might all be suffering from something curable, so I advised them to see a doctor. They assured me that no doctor could help—it was nature's verdict, they believed. All that could be done, they maintained, was to hold oneself in while making love, to avoid thinking about the woman, to avoid concentrating on what one was doing, feeling or wanting to feel.

They complained that a woman seldom if ever tells a man how he compares with other men with whom she has been intimate; she fears revealing herself. This is a barrier, they argued. A man is condemned never to know himself as a lover.

I recalled the girl friend I had when I was in high school. We used to make love when my parents were out. One day the telephone rang during our love-making; since it stood on the night table, I answered it without interrupting our love-making and talked for a while to the friend who had called. When I hung up, the girl told me she would never make love with me again.

It upset her, she said, that I could have an erection purely through an act of will—as though I had only to stretch my leg or bend a finger. She stressed the idea of spontaneity, claiming I should have a sense of wanting, of sudden desire. I told her it didn't matter, but she insisted it did, claiming that if I made a conscious decision to have an erection, it would reduce the act of making love to something very mechanical and ordinary.

•

In the first days of the month the regiment started its preparations for the National Day parade, and several hundred of us, chosen for our uniform height and familiarity with parade-ground drill, began our daily rehearsals.

We used to muster at dawn on the packed, sun-baked earth of the parade ground, surrounded by forest. Despite the summer heat the drills lasted all day, and we marched up and down in a single column four abreast, goose-stepping along the whole length of the parade ground, all six units wheeling and turning, crossing and recrossing each other's tracks like so many shunting railroad cars.

After a month of this arduous training we had become a single entity, marching as one man. We breathed in unison and saluted with a single gesture; we swung our rifles that had become an extension of our bones and muscles. All that we could think of during those exhausting days was the pain of our swollen, burning feet, and our warm, coarse uniforms rubbing against our sweaty skins. It seemed we were forever marching toward the motionless forest, but invariably the column would turn about before reaching the shadow of the trees.

On National Day reveille came earlier than usual. The parade was to be held some distance from the camp. It was then I realized that I could miss the entire tedious day. If four of us, the three men who marched abreast of me and I, should quietly disappear and spend the rest of the day in the forest, it would be extremely unlikely that our overanxious officers would detect our absence. In the evening we could easily re-enter the camp and lose ourselves among the returning soldiers.

I spoke to my fellow soldiers; they agreed to the plan and we decided to leave the camp before the first muster was called. Instead of going to breakfast in the canteen we marched over to the dumping ground, as though we were the men attached to the sanitation detail. Then it was merely a matter of affecting the confidence to stand about at the loading platform and signal the trucks in and out, until a suitable moment would present itself to walk off into the forest. We were not challenged, and as soon as we had burst through the first bushes, we began to run, dragging our rifles. The jays screamed as we plunged ahead, and occasional squirrels leaped from bough to bough ahead of us. We were deep in the forest before stopping. We stripped and lay down.

As the sun climbed higher, the forest floor steamed. A single distant bugle call broke into the myriad sounds of chirping and buzzing that drifted into the clearing. We fell asleep.

When I awoke I felt heavy, my throat burned; I grew more alert and stood up. The sun touched the treetops, the light in the clearing was dim. My fellow absentees were still asleep, their uniforms hanging on the nearby bushes. A sound was approaching from the depths of the forest: it was getting louder and closer every second. Suddenly I realized that it was the band. I peered in the direction of the sound. What I saw shocked me: less than two hundred yards away our regimental band was marching through the trees toward us, the bandleader's gilded staff flashing as it caught the light, the white leather aprons of the drummers standing out clearly against the green of the foliage.

I sprang to my uniform, for a moment thinking only of making a run for cover. Then I jumped over to my lazily stretched-out companions and shook them from their sleep as they mumbled abuse at me. When they finally grasped what was about to happen, the same panic hit them. They grabbed their uniforms, boots and rifles, and plunged into the tangle of bushes and trees.

Impulsively I threw myself forward, and was instantly gripped by an immobilizing tremor. Within seconds the seizure passed, but I still could not flee. I simply stood in the clearing, naked, my rifle and uniform at my feet, as though I had consciously decided to hold my ground and wait for the column to arrive.

The leading ranks were only yards away. They had now perceived me, for the band stopped playing and several mounted officers detached themselves from the body of the troops and galloped toward the clearing.

There was pandemonium in the column; some men had broken ranks and others were shouting and gesturing at me. The regimental standard swung into sight and I was possessed by the reflex to salute. I reached for my cap, drew myself to attention, and raised my hand to my brow. A derisive cry went up from the nearest soldiers, a single bugler raised his instrument and gave a hunting call, breaking the sequence of my movements. I stared down in horror at myself: there was nothing I could do—I was aroused.

Commands rang out: the column halted, and though the sergeants ordered the men to hold their ranks, they could not prevent them from laughing. Two soldiers advanced toward me, followed by a mounted officer. A second officer dismounted and bellowed that I was under arrest. Other commands were given: the column re-formed and marched off, continuing on its short cut through the glade to the camp. I dressed and was led away by the guards.

I was charged with absenting myself without leave and with deserting my place of duty. I was called upon to name my companions; but I stated I had acted entirely alone, maintaining they must have arrived in the clearing independently while I was asleep. I insisted that I was guilty only of the minor charge of not signing out of the camp, claiming that I had been released from the parade during a drill by one of the officers; and though he no longer chose to recall it, my absence should not be held against me. To the charge that my salute, when naked, was a studied insult to the flag, I pointed out that there had been many occasions when soldiers who were caught naked by surprise attack had been compelled to fight in such a state.

●

Are you circumcised? I've always wondered. Not that I'm sure I would know the difference anyway.

Why didn't you ask me before?

It's really not that it's important, and I was afraid to ask the question. You might have interpreted it as some sort of expectation on my part, even as disapproval. Aren't men very sensitive about things like this?

I don't know; men vary.

Is circumcision really necessary? Like having your appendix out, for instance?

No, it isn't.

Today it seems so cruel and unnecessary; a part of an infant's body is removed without his consent! Isn't it possible that as a result of mutilating him, the man becomes less sensitive and responsive? After all, a delicate organ that nature intended to be covered and kept tender becomes exposed, and almost like one's knees and elbows, is constantly chafed by the linen, wool, and cotton one wears . . .

●

I was ordered to camouflage myself in a forest several miles from any settlement. I selected a full-branched tree and prepared a comfortable perch, remaining there for several hours during the maneuvers. Scanning the surroundings through my field glasses I noticed another camouflaged soldier from my regiment, positioned about half a mile away. Since I had been ordered not to reveal my position, I remained hidden, looking at him occasionally through my binoculars. Suddenly I was alerted by his movement and followed the arc of his rifle barrel: on the border of a distant field, just outside the boundaries of the regiment's territory, two people were walking slowly. The soldier's rifle kicked twice and muffled shots cut into the silence. When I looked at the couple again, they lay in the swaying grass like two surfers abruptly swept off their boards by an unpredictable wave.

I watched the sniper closely now. Though I could not see his face, it occurred to me that he might have seen and recognized me, and I felt my heart contract; but his rifle lay across his knees and he lolled peacefully against the boughs that gave with the drowsy sway of the forest. I peered at him cautiously until the bluish air drooped over the scraggly trees, and darkness rose as though born from the dew which covered the ground.

The next day the adjutant announced that two civilians had been killed by stray gunfire. The investigation did not produce any results, since we were all able to account for our allotted ammunition.

Later two truckloads of regimental soccer players took a short cut through a field reserved for artillery practice. The field was supposed to be marked as a danger area, but either the drivers did not see the warning signs or someone in the regiment had removed the signs; in any case, the soccer players never arrived. The trucks must have traveled halfway across the field when the artillery opened fire: all that was left was a pair of surprisingly clean white tennis shoes.

S UPPOSE HE WOULD BECOME *my lover? To kill
that thought you'd have to destroy him, wouldn't you?*

I don't know. I'm not sure.

*Once, when we were buying a coat for me, the
salesman came over to help me try it on. When he put
his hand on my neck to adjust the collar, you came up to
him and without a word took his hand and removed it—
just as though it were an object. You must have squeezed
his hand terribly hard: he froze. His face was almost pur-*

ple and his mouth opened as if he were going to cry out.

I took his hand off your neck because I didn't want him to touch you.

He certainly didn't mean to be personal.

I don't know what he meant and you don't either. I was thinking about what you might be feeling when he touched you.

To kill your thought you actually had to remove his hand from my neck?

Yes.

Could you kill a man? I mean: for some important reason?

I don't know.

●

Work was scarce during the war; I was too thin to work in the fields, and the peasants preferred to use their own children or relatives on the farms. As a vagrant, I was everybody's victim. To amuse himself the farmer with whom I was finally boarded would take hold of me by my collar, drag me up close and then strike me. Sometimes he would call his brother or his friends to share in a game in which I had to stand still—staring ahead with open eyes—while they stood a few paces in front of me and spat at my face, betting on how often they could hit me in the eye.

This spitting game became very popular in the village. I was a target for everyone—little boys and girls, farmers and their wives, sober men and drunkards.

One day I attended the funeral of a child who had died of mushroom poisoning, the son of one of the richest farmers in the village. Everybody who came to the funeral was dressed in his Sunday best, looking meek and humble.

I watched the mourning father as he stood at the open grave. His face was yellow as the newly turned earth, his eyes red and swollen. He leaned on his wife, his legs unsteady, barely able to bear his weight. When the coffin was brought to the graveside he threw himself on the polished lid, babbling and kissing it as though it were his child. His cries and those of his wife broke the silence, like a chorus on an empty stage.

It became clear to me that the peasants' love for their children was just as uncontrollable as an outbreak of fever among the cattle. Often I saw a mother touching her child's soft hair, a father's hands flinging the child into the air and catching it safely again. Frequently I watched the small children wobbling on their plump legs, stumbling, falling, getting up again, as though borne up by the same force that steadies sunflowers buffeted by the wind.

Then one day I saw a sheep writhing convulsively in a slow death, its desperate bleating bringing terror to the entire flock. The peasants claimed that the animal must have swallowed a fishhook or a shard of glass in its feed.

Months passed. One morning a cow from the

herd in my charge strayed onto a neighbor's property, damaging the crops. This was reported to my master. Upon my return from the fields, the farmer was waiting for me. He pushed me into the barn and whipped me until the blood oozed from my legs. Bellowing with rage he finally hurled the leather thong into my face.

I began to collect discarded fishhooks and bury them behind the barn. After the farmer and his wife left for church I slipped into my hiding place and kneaded a couple of fishhooks and crushed glass into balls of fresh bread which I had torn out of the day's newly baked loaves.

I liked to play with the youngest of the farmer's three children. We often met in the farmyard, and she would laugh uproariously while I imitated a frog or a stork.

One evening the little girl hugged me. I dampened a ball of bread with my saliva and asked her to swallow it in one piece. When she hesitated, I took a piece of apple, put it into the back of my mouth, and pushing it with my forefinger, instantly swallowed it. The girl imitated me, swallowing the balls, one after another. I looked away from her face, forcing myself to think only of the burning of her father's whip.

From then on I gazed boldly into my persecutors' eyes, provoking their assault and maltreatment. I felt no pain. For each lash I received my tormentors were condemned to pain a hundred times greater than mine. Now I was no longer their victim; I had become their judge and executioner.

There were no doctors or hospitals in the area

—the nearest railway only carried an occasional freight train. At dawn crying parents carried their gasping children to the church so the priest could purify them with holy water. But at dusk, in a more desperate mood, they took the dying to the distant huts of the local witches who practiced sorcery and healing.

But death continued to levy its toll, and children went on dying. Some of the peasants blasphemed God, whispering it was He Himself who had dispatched His only son, Jesus, to inevitable crucifixion, in order to redeem His own sin of creating so cruel a world. Others insisted that Death had come to dwell in the villages to avoid the bombed cities, and the war, and the camps where the furnaces smoked day and night.

●

There was a man at the university who had wronged me. I discovered he was of peasant stock and therefore privileged among those whom the Party had pushed into the university for political reasons. I could not change the climate which favored him and thus saw no way of countering his enmity. It occurred to me that to blame the system was simply an excuse which prevented my facing him.

At that time we were all required to join the para-military student defense corps. Every unit in turn had to guard the university arsenal, which was under the jurisdiction of the city garrison. We regularly had a two-day guard duty, which was organized along military lines: the guards' quarters occupied a wing of the university and were run like an army barracks. Telephone messages had to be recorded and acted upon as set forth in the military manuals, and instructions had to be followed with the utmost precision, since, as we were often warned, the city military commander might at any time declare a full-scale alert to test the efficiency of the student defense corps.

One day I observed this man reverently acknowledging instructions from the headquarters of the university arsenal, his knuckles tense and white as he gripped the telephone receiver. I looked at him closely again. I now had a plan.

By the time he was appointed guard commander for a weekend, I had already spent many hours practicing a brusque military voice, smart with clipped arrogance. On his first day of duty I telephoned him at midnight, and in the most urgent and authoritative tones announced I was the city garrison duty-officer and that I wished to speak directly to the guard commander. In my assumed voice I proceeded to inform him that an army exercise was in progress, and that in accordance with the plan, he was to muster the university unit and move through the park for a surprise attack on the city arsenal. Once there, his unit was to disarm the regular guards, force an entry and take over the building until the exercise was called off. I asked him to give the instructions back to me: he excitedly repeated my orders, obviously failing to register the omission of the daily password, which I could not give him.

When half an hour later I telephoned the post again, there was no answer: his unit had probably left to storm the arsenal.

On Monday all of us heard about what had happened. Exactly as I had intended, his unit had advanced and attacked the arsenal. In the garrison a full-scale alert had been set off, since it was assumed that there was either a mutinous invasion under way, a counterrevolution, or some secret regional exercise. The university unit was promptly rounded up and arrested; its commander was charged with armed insurrection.

During the court-martial he insisted that backed by the password he had acted under direct orders from the city's garrison. He clung pathetically to his story.

●

She said she was the only girl in the family, but that she had an older brother. He liked her very much, she said, the two of them hardly ever quarreled. But he seemed to like only the boys she wasn't interested in, and he became quite difficult when she was with someone she really liked. He would follow her then, and it was obvious that he didn't intend to leave her alone with any man. He provoked fights with the young men who danced with her or who embraced or attempted to kiss her. He often acted as though he were her boy friend himself. Yet, she said, she was proud of him. He was very good-looking and the best student in his class. And many girls fell in love with him.

At one time she had a boy friend who told her that he thought her brother and she were made of the same substance and that theirs was the temperament to which he was most strongly attracted. Her brother, he said, was an extension of her, and she an extension of him. He added that being in love with her meant also being emotionally involved with her brother.

She realized that she and her brother could become allies against the rest of the world. They should choose each other, she said, they should become attached and committed to each other, and they could still treat their relation as an experiment; if it didn't work out, she said, then they could blame their failure on the fact that they were brother and sister. But if it did work out, it would be so comfortable, so convenient. She didn't see anything unnatural about such a relationship; certainly there was more of a difference between her brother and her than, say, between two women who fall in love with each other and have the physical relationship she had come across so often in college. It would be an alliance unlike one she could have with anyone else. The two of them could do or say whatever they pleased; she could never be so free, or so much herself, with any other person.

•

I telephoned her after my return, but she wasn't at home. Finally I reached her and arranged to meet her for lunch. She plied me with all the usual questions: How had the trip been? What had I done? Where had I stayed? Whom had I met? . . . I gave her a full account and then asked what she had been doing in the city during the past few days.

She told me that she had gone to the baths to keep the appointment I had made for her. She had been expecting a masseuse, but there she was told that the masseur I had sent was waiting. She felt very uneasy, she said, but didn't want to embarrass me by refusing him.

But why did you send a man? Did you have any particular reason?

None besides the massage. Did you enjoy it?

He was very efficient. He seemed to know exactly what he was doing.

Then you have no complaints?

None.

Why did you feel so uneasy?

There was something he was doing which I didn't know how to accept.

But you did accept it?

I had no choice. All I could have done was to leave.

Did you leave?

No, I stayed for the whole session.

Did you say anything to him? No, you allowed his hands to do whatever they were doing.

The way you say that makes me feel you knew in advance what he would try to do. If that is so, why did you choose him?

I wanted to know what you would do: how you would behave in that sort of situation.

How I would behave? Don't you think it was far more important for you to prevent him from behaving as he did? After all, you know me very well.

I sent him to you on purpose, because I know his hands. Tell me, did you get any relief?

They were not his hands any more. Somehow, during the massage, the thought occurred to me they were your hands. I suppose that's what you really wanted.

Over coffee I suddenly sprang a question: I asked whether she had met anyone interesting while I was away. She looked straight at me without answering and only pursed her lips. Then she admitted without any embarrassment that she had been seeing a man.

Indeed? What's he like?

There's nothing to say about him. I spent some time with him. That's why I wasn't home when you phoned me.

I see. But you wrote me that you'd been staying overnight with your friends.

I was lying.

So you were seeing a man. For how long?

/ 43

Only for two weeks.

Every day?

Practically.

Did you meet him before I left?

No. I met him just after the last time you phoned, when you said that you wanted us to live together. I went to a party. Someone introduced him. I saw him the following night, and the next, and the next.

Why are you telling me about it?

I would feel awkward hiding it from you. I don't want to be separated from you by an experience you know nothing about. You see, after you told me you wanted us to live together, I had to find out whether I could still be interested in someone else, and whether someone else would appreciate me as much as you do. I felt I had an obligation to know myself better—apart from the self you have brought me to know. I thought I might be completely bound to you simply because you had influenced me so much. Then, when you went away, I felt as if I had a judge and jury inside me, and I had to answer to them in order to justify my choice of a man to live with, and the kind of love I could give and receive.

So to find out whether you loved me, you had to sleep with another man?

I didn't sleep with him.

But if you wanted to find out how you are without me, why did you refuse such a critical test?

I didn't refuse; he didn't ask me. He said he loved me and wanted to marry me. Maybe he thought that if he asked me to go to bed with him, I would refuse because of my involvement with you. You see, I told him about you, and what was between us.

But you spent a lot of time together. He must have kissed you. You touched him.

Yes.

And his tongue was in your mouth, and he stroked your body. Tell me, would you have gone to bed with him if he had wanted you to?

I was ready to.

What is the verdict of your judge and jury?

The verdict is that I am capable of independent judgment and that I want to remain with you.

And him?

I told him I wouldn't leave you. I like him; he's a good man; but it would be a different life with him. I know I prefer the life you and I have together. I chose that part of me which wants you over and above the self I would become with him. Above all, I know that I alone decided this.

•

By the way, there's something I hid from you.

What is it?

It's simple—well, not quite so simple. Some

weeks ago I was talking to the manager of the detective agency that investigates and protects the clients of the firm I work for. I asked him how people were watched and what the procedure was. Was surveillance really effective or just a sort of bogus cloak-and-dagger operation? I accepted the manager's offer to try out the services of his agency by allowing myself to be followed. He, in turn, would test his employees by comparing his detectives' reports with mine. The results were gratifying to both of us: every meeting I had with you—time, place, duration—was recorded. And then, when I went away, you, as my prime contact, were watched, and quite efficiently too. Every meeting you had with that man was recorded. Yet you still deny that you slept with him, that you spent your nights together.

It doesn't mean that I slept with him just because I spent a night in his apartment.

But since you spent several nights there, it's not too much to assume that he made love to you or—if you prefer—that you gave yourself to him?

I don't deny it, but an act of intercourse is not a commitment unless it stems from a particular emotion and a certain frame of mind. It wasn't an act based on love; but I had to make sure, in order to discover myself, whether it would lead to love.

You speak of your love-making with him as though it were a sort of planned program.

That's not so—I had to like him.

I didn't realize that you liked each other. I see. You both wanted each other, and there was the usual

/ 46

warmth and intimate caresses, each one impatiently waiting for the other to come.

Yes, but it could not be planned. I liked him;
it was spontaneous. And because it was that, it became a
good test: it answered the questions I asked myself.

I WON A PRIZE in a photographic contest sponsored by a society for the aid of the old and infirm, and I was commissioned to supply the society with a collection of portraits. The photographs were supposed to depict the serenity and peace of old age. I was required to make up a portfolio of sixty portraits, but I encountered great difficulty in finding suitable subjects. There were very few elderly people left in the cities because the government had set up homes for them in the rural districts.

To reach the nearest home, I had to make a difficult journey, laden with flood lamps, film, cables, transformers, and screens. I also took a portable darkroom so that I could determine on the spot the results of my work. When I arrived, the director of the home showed me around. It was an enormous old manor house converted into a score of wards, eight beds in each. All the patients here were aged, and the majority of them were also sickly, crippled, or senile. It occurred to me immediately that the task I was about to attempt was far more difficult than I had imagined. I was surrounded, pushed, pulled, spat on and cursed by some of these old people, and, on occasion, physically soiled. The wards with public toilets were dark and poorly ventilated. There was an oppressive stench of sweat and urine, against which no disinfectant could make headway.

The next day I returned with my cameras and equipment. Some of the patients I selected refused to pose, claiming they were blinded by the spotlights; others, shaking and spitting, crowded in front of my camera to flaunt their wrinkled, flabby bodies, pulling back their lips and drooling through shrunken and toothless gums. Still others tried to cut the cables running from the electric sockets to the lights; they stepped on my equipment, kicked at the tripod, or plucked at me with hands smeared with excrement. I was unable to take a single successful picture, and one of my cameras was broken. Just before retiring to my quarters I stopped at the director's office.

While I waited, a nurse came into the room. After sipping a glass of water she sank wearily into a chair, and although I had been staring at her she ignored me completely. I felt an urge to touch her face and hair and to smell her skin. I did not care whether or not she was beautiful; it was enough that she was clean and healthy. I desperately wanted to reassure myself that I had nothing in common with the inmates. If she would be willing to help me, I knew I could complete my work.

Abruptly she acknowledged me, asking if I was visiting a relative. When I told her about my project, she reluctantly agreed to work with me, if the director was willing.

The director agreed to assign her to me for the next few days, adding casually that she was a student of psychology. She was especially interested in the psychological problems of the aged and the retarded, so much so that she had requested an additional year's training before taking her degree. Almost three years had passed, and she was still there, working as chief nurse. According to him, she was completely devoted to the patients.

We started photographing early next morning. Our presence in the wards continued to create difficulties. Many of the male patients tried to attract the nurse's attention with inviting gestures; the women, on the other hand, tried to upset her with offensive remarks. She told me it was only to be expected.

When interruptions made work impossible, I would move toward her and put my arm on her shoulder or let my hand brush against her hair as I bent down to pick up a lens from its case. She showed no sign of embarrassment. I continued to touch her whenever our work gave me the occasion.

There was nothing to do outside the home: the local village was small and the nearest town was forty miles away. We had no cinema, no theater, no restaurant.

Apparently my companion was without friends. The rest of the staff was middle-aged, either married or, from her point of view, unsuitable. She mentioned a boy friend in the navy, to whom she wrote regularly.

She was a secretive person, giving no reason for staying so long at the institution and no explanation for not returning to the university to finish her studies. All she said was that her life was her own. Her complacency irritated me. I began to resent the fact that my presence made no difference to her, that she could endure for years an environment which I found unbearable even for a few days. To her, perhaps, there was nothing different or unusual about me. I might have been just another patient, merely a little younger, a little less decrepit than the others.

I began finding certain points of similarity between myself and the inmates. Nor could I avoid the realization that one day I would become what they were now, that the forces which had reduced them to their present state would also take me prisoner. I watched the sick in their endless torment, crawling like broken crayfish. As I worked in the wards I saw the dying inmates, rheumy-eyed and hollow-faced, their bodies shrunken by disease, lying on their narrow beds gaping apathetically at the faded portraits of saints or at the wooden crucifixes stippled with wormholes. Some clutched photographs of their children.

In moments like these I would turn away and stare at the girl for a long while. So complete was my illusion of possessing her that I would experience the most intense rapture amid the most commonplace distractions.

It was always the same. She would help me to pack my equipment and store it for the next day; then she would leave. One afternoon, however, I left the ward and walked down to the basement. I knew she was there. The basement was cold and damp and I stood in darkness. She called my name; I moved toward her voice.

I touched her uniform and knelt in front of her. I lifted her skirt. The starched fabric crackled. She was naked beneath; I pressed my face into her, my body throbbing with the force which makes trees reach upward to drive out blossoms from small, shrunken buds. I was young.

One evening I decided to surprise her with a visit. When I reached her room the other occupant told me she was on the fourth floor of the building. Only as I turned away from her room did it occur to me that I had never been on the fourth floor, which was used mainly for storage. It was quiet when I reached the stairs. Alert to everything, I mounted cautiously, and when the staircase opened into the hallway I found myself facing an ironbound door leading into a narrow, windowless corridor. Inside, it was dark. For a moment I trailed my hands over the walls. There were grates on each side of the passage, but they were all bolted. Then I noticed a single shaft of light escaping from under a door at the far end of the hall. Before I could reach it, I heard her voice. As I moved closer, I stumbled over a small sandbag and crashed against the door. Even as I clutched at the lintel I was halfway into the room.

She was lying naked on the bed, half covered by the furry body of a creature with a human head, paw-like hands, and the short, barrel-chested trunk of an ape. My rapid, blundering entrance frightened them: the creature turned, its small brown eyes glittering maliciously. With a single leap it reached its crib, and whining and yelping, began to burrow under the covers.

The girl pitched forward, her thighs closing as though to protect herself. Her trembling hands searched about her like the claws of a dying chicken; she clutched her dress and begun pulling it over her belly. I thought for a moment that she would crawl into the wall or scuttle through the floor boards. Her eyes looked stony and unfocused; a broken word rose to her lips, but she was unable to utter it. I stared at the crib and realized that the creature in it was human. Turning, I put out the light.

I hurried to my cottage in the village and immediately started to fill the bath. Sitting back in the warm water, I could hear only the measured dripping of the tap.

●

I can't make love to you now. Why do you insist?

    I want to make love to you when you're menstruating. It's as though a part of me were caught in you and your blood were mine, pulsing out from a vein that belongs to us both. What do you feel then?

    I feel the blood staining our bodies as if your hardness made me bleed, as if you had flayed my skin, and had eaten me, and I was drained.

●

The girl and I were talking under the dark shrubbery of the park when our path was blocked by four men. We quickly turned aside, but heard others breaking through the bushes a few steps behind us. They called out to one another, and I realized that they were in collusion with those we had seen on the path. I was sure that we would be attacked and robbed unless we could meet other strollers or find a place to hide. I knew where we were: a stream lay ahead, and I recalled a deserted gazebo, once a lovers' rendezvous, behind the bushes that lined the bank. We stooped to push our way through the spiky dwarf pines, shielding our faces from the sharp branches.

I thought for a moment that we had escaped our pursuers, but suddenly we heard their voices again. They had only paused at the edge of the pine copse.

We reached the gazebo and crawled into the narrow space between its foundation and a stack of benches. But our pursuers crashed through the pines and found us. Instantly a dozen hands pulled at us. We were dragged to our feet. The girl gave a desperate cry; as I turned, a blow stunned me.

When I came to, I could see the men tearing off the girl's clothing. She fought, kicking and biting. I braced myself and almost managed to get up, but the men pushed my head back against the ground. I looked toward the girl: she had been forced down on her back, her legs flailing; they were upraised and spread apart, like oars suspended above the water before striking.

The men assaulted her, their trousers tangled around their ankles, their jackets thrown over the nearby bushes. They took turns. Those still waiting turned their flashlights on her writhing body. Then they began to act in concert, several of them bending over her at once, gripping and kneading her flesh, locking her head between their thighs. She no longer screamed; I heard only her broken gasps and occasional sobs. Then she vomited and was silent.

When the men had done, they released me and ran off. They were snickering to each other and calling out obscenities, as their voices died away among the trees and the dark walks and alleys. At last I was able to pull myself to my feet, aware that my only injuries were a spinning head and pain in breathing. I went over to my friend and picked up the remnants of her clothes. I helped her to a bench near the stream. She fell back shivering, her breath hot and sour. She moved her hands over her body, her fingers tracing the scratches and bruises which had been inflicted on her. I struck a match and caught a glimpse of her haggard face, the dark bruises on her chest, the streaks of blood on her thighs and hips.

We made our way slowly along the bank of the stream until we reached the open ground and the park exit. We turned into a dimly lit road. A policeman cycling past stopped just ahead of us. My friend whispered urgently to me to say nothing, and clutching her torn dress, she jumped off the path into the shadows. The policeman informed us that the park closed at dusk and that we were committing an offense by remaining there.

As we walked on I felt an increasing apprehension, realizing she expected to spend the night with me. I wondered whether there would be any change in her when we made love in the future. Of course, I very much regretted what had happened to her, but a sense of revulsion was also beginning to settle in me. I still saw her flattened on the damp earth, her legs spread apart, her body plumbed and polluted by others. I couldn't think of her except as a body to make love to.

Early in the morning she went to the clinic for an examination. I hoped she would recover soon, so we could again make love. I reminded myself that I would have to be tender and gentle to her, but the thought was unwelcome. I recalled watching a ballerina whose skill and balance I admired; when I learned that she was pregnant, I could not avoid imagining her unborn child thrown about inside her with every leap she made.

The girl spent two days in the clinic, and after she was released she came immediately to me. She undressed to show me that the bruises had almost disappeared and then took a shower while I prepared the bed.

Afraid to show any reluctance, I took her rapidly, before she was ready. She moaned and then collected herself, begging me to do what we had done so many times before, things I could not bring myself to do with her now. Afterward she asked me why I had been so violent. I told her the truth. Our relationship had changed.

Her moods were fitful: she was either pensive and quiet, or exuberant and nervously excited, assuring me again and again that the doctors had given her a clean bill of health. She stressed the phrase—"as though nothing had happened"—attempting with difficulty to nullify the rape during which, she insisted, she had been numb and felt nothing.

In my dreams I saw her emerging from a shell, twitching and quivering, creeping closer and closer until she touched me. Then suddenly each of us became male and female at the same time, seeking each other's orifices and rearing up back to back, wounding each other with our organs, tumbling to the ground to discharge blood in rapid climaxes.

My curiosity about her body intensified. Abruptly and forcefully I subjected her to various experiments, stimulating her responses, exploring and violating

/ 57

her in spite of her pleas and protests. She became an object which I could control or pair with other objects. I didn't hesitate to employ artificial devices to arouse her or to sustain her excitement. She attributed the change in my behavior to the rape, and she demanded to know whether I was hating and punishing her or myself for what had happened. She wondered whether my new urgency was a disguise for the love which she claimed I was now ashamed to show her.

One evening she mentioned a neighbor of hers, a girl, who was attracted to her and who had made several attempts to be intimate with her. I told her to invite this girl to share in our love-making. I explained that her neighbor did not interest me as a woman, but merely as another kind of object with which I could excite her and therefore myself even more. Surprisingly, she made no protest and called her.

A few days later they both appeared; I noticed that her neighbor carried an overnight bag. I made it clear to our guest that she was free to employ any means she wanted to arouse my friend, but that I would come between them whenever I wanted. I pointed out that I had made their intimacy possible for my sake, and that she must comply. She agreed to spend the weekend with us.

In the weeks that followed, my friend began to drink, and I decided not to discourage her: alcohol made her an even more responsive subject. Now her passiveness kept me actively preoccupied with her.

One of my friends was planning a party for some of his male colleagues. On the evening of the party my girl friend began drinking, obviously resentful that I intended to go without her. Finally I offered to take her along.

The party was well under way when we arrived. She had no hesitation toasting each of the guests. I noted the easy familiarity with which she embraced my friends and her provocative, almost flaunting remarks. I realized that she would soon become an embarrassment to me; I felt trapped.

In the next half hour I approached each of the men and whispered that the girl was my gift to the host and to his guests; if they would devise the situation, each could have his pleasure.

The excitement increased: the girl began surrounding herself with the more boisterous guests. Amid a burst of laughter, I saw her being raised shoulder-high, her dress awry, her legs wrapped around the neck of the man whose head she clasped. As I watched, a dozen hands stretched up past her thighs to feel her belly and her breasts. She gave a sudden cry. The pearl necklace I once had given her snapped, and the tiny iridescent seeds cascaded down, lost now in the swaying, heaving rush that carried her toward the bedroom. I left.

●

These girls so carefully posed in the windows are prostitutes, aren't they?

Yes, they are.

In other neighborhoods the prostitutes walk the streets and use hotel rooms, yet here they have their own apartments.

The girls don't own the apartments, they simply rent them. Often two or three of them use the same place, taking turns by day or night.

Do they like working that way?

Yes, they please the man who is disturbed by the crudeness of the streetwalker and the necessity of approaching her on the street and of following her to a hotel in full view of others. But these women at the windows suggest something else: their apartments mean privacy and comfort; doors can be locked, curtains drawn. A man can see himself as a guest in a home and the girl as his hostess. He comes in order to relax and without any particular motive. Then whatever happens seems more natural.

Have you ever been with a prostitute?

Yes.

Before you met me or since?

That can't make any difference.

But why would you want a prostitute? What could she do that I don't? Is she more willing than I am?

I do with her what you would find unacceptable.

How do you know I would?

Because you know me only in a certain way. And because our relationship is based on your acceptance of what I have been with you.

/ 60

Then what I assume to be you is only one side of you.

You also offer only the side of yourself which you think is most acceptable to me. So far neither of us has revealed anything which contradicts what we have both always assumed.

When you are with a prostitute, whatever she does or says is pretense; she wants your money, not you.

Money extends my potency; without it I couldn't be what I am. I wouldn't be able to meet you where I do and in the fashion I do. I wouldn't be living the way I do, nor could I afford the experiences I require.

Still, whatever a prostitute does with you she also does with others, doesn't she? Doesn't that make you jealous?

It doesn't concern me: the knowledge that other men have her is not disturbing in her case. So many others possess her that they do not amount to rivals. In a way, one even feels a sort of sympathy with them, because one's choice of a prostitute is confirmed by those who have had her before. Since no man is excluded from having her, she appears to be not so much a woman as a desire that all men share in common.

But after you leave her, she isn't even aware that you exist.

When I leave her, the awareness of what has happened leaves with me: that awareness is mine, not hers.

I FOUND HIM ATTRACTIVE *and charming. He spoke with an accent; I think he's a foreigner.*

He is. He came to this country some years ago. But he's here permanently now.

Do you know him well?

Yes.

What does he do?

He's an architect. He designs highly func-

tional buildings, where style is only secondary: hospitals, schools, prisons, funeral parlors, clinics for animals.

Funeral parlors?

Certainly. They have to be built, too, you know, just like maternity clinics.

But that's so unusual.

Not really. He once told me that in the late thirties, just after he graduated from the university, he worked for a firm of architects. His first assignment was to draw up plans for a concentration camp.

He refused.

No, he didn't. Even though it was difficult, because there were so few precedents, but that made it all the more challenging. He told me that at that time many architects were competing for projects sponsored by the government. Of course, when they were designing a school or hospital or even a prison he and his colleagues could easily imagine themselves inside it, but a concentration camp was entirely different: it required exceptional vision. Still, there was something of the school about it, of the hospital, the waiting rooms in public buildings, and something of the funeral home also, only the section for disposing of the bodies was more efficient. Above all, it had to be functional; this was the underlying philosophy. He had carefully taken the terrain into account: one style of camp for a broken belt of rolling foothills and another for a treeless, steppe-like country. Since abundant funds and land were available, my friend's designs were promptly accepted. Nevertheless, it was just a project. You could look at it from many points of view: in a maternity hospital, for instance, more people leave than arrive; in a concentration camp the reverse is true. Its main purpose is hygiene.

Hygiene? What do you mean?

Have you ever seen rats being exterminated? Or, better—do you like animals?

Of course.

Well, rats are also animals.

Not really. I mean they're not domestic animals. They're dangerous, and therefore they have to be exterminated.

Exactly: they have to be exterminated; it's a problem of hygiene. Rats have to be removed. We exterminate them, but this has nothing to do with our attitudes toward cats, dogs, or any other animal. Rats aren't murdered—we get rid of them; or, to use a better word, they are eliminated; this act of elimination is empty of all meaning. There's no ritual in it, no symbolism; the right of the executioner is never questioned. That's why in the concentration camps my friend designed, the victims never remained individuals; they became as identical as rats. They existed only to be killed.

●

I followed the river to my friend's lodgings. It was years since we had last met and only by chance that I learned he was living in the city. A few buildings clustered around what passed for a square; others straggled along the canals and the railroad tracks. Below his house a cemetery bordered the river.

I walked toward the cemetery, knowing I would see him as he returned home. Already I could feel neglect hovering over the graves.

Within minutes I heard my name called, and looked up to see my friend hurrying down from the road. He seemed amused that I had chosen to wait for him in the cemetery, adding that the place looked derelict from not having been used for so many years. The inscriptions on the headstones were barely legible, and many of the stones had sunk drunkenly into the ground. The people buried there, he said, constituted a religious minority who for a long time had not been allowed to bury their dead within the city limits, because their funeral processions incited the townspeople to attack them. The bodies were therefore transported here on boats.

But, he went on, it was not the graves that were interesting; it was the caretaker. My friend said he had spoken to him many times, but hadn't got more than the briefest responses. His curiosity aroused, he had inquired about him from the people of the town.

According to them, the caretaker had been interned in a concentration camp during the war. Before that, he had been a heavyweight boxer; although no champion, he had been well known in boxing circles for his tremendous strength. Few managers would risk handling him because he had injured and crippled several of his opponents. The concentration-camp commandant had noticed the man while making selections for the gas chambers and decided to keep him as a private sparring partner for himself and for the guards who liked to box.

The commandant invited a professional boxer to challenge the prisoner. He decided that both boxers would have to fight as hard as they would in a championship bout. If the prisoner-champion won the match, an extra prisoner would be executed. If he happened to be outpointed or knocked out, he could ask for the release of a single prisoner otherwise destined for the gas chamber. But he had to fight honestly, without exposing himself needlessly to his opponent and without pretending to lose strength or get groggy. If he were suspected of losing intentionally, he would be put to death.

The commandant, who prided himself on his insight into the prison mentality and the survival instinct, obviously assumed that his prisoner-champion would fight well in order to stay alive and yet would not be overanxious for a victory which would condemn one of his fellow prisoners to the ovens. Deprived of the will to conquer he would still have to fight to win.

When the professional arrived, it seemed probable that the prisoner would be defeated. Unfortunately for the commandant, the visiting boxer, faced with the choice of losing the contest to a prisoner, an enemy of his race, or winning it only to release another such enemy from death, refused to fight. The prisoner survived, unable to save anyone but himself.

Now he lived alone, watching the headstones steadily sinking into the fetid mud.

When I was attending the university, there were numerous obligatory meetings of the many student political organizations. During the lengthy sessions the students were required by the Party to evaluate each other and themselves. The meetings were tense and often dramatic: if a student's progress or conduct was assessed unfavorably, the Party could remove him from the university and assign him to a job deep in some remote province. It was as if each of us were a stone resting in a slingshot; we never knew who would launch us, or where to.

Just before a meeting I went to the lavatory. There I ran into another student, nicknamed "The Philosopher," who looked haggard and began to vomit in uncontrollable spasms. When he saw me he tried to excuse himself and even attempted a smile.

He found these meetings unbearable; he was far too nervous to handle the strain. He told me that a room crowded with people triggered off a panic in him, and he often spent hours alone in the corridors, trying to calm himself before returning to the classroom.

One day I was late for an appointment with him. I explained that I had been delayed by a visit to the new state bank which had just opened a branch in the center of the city. In an offhand way I told him that on the ground floor there were imposing lavatories, all clean and as yet scarcely used. I said I had visited them.

My friend became intensely interested, asking

for the exact location of the bank. When I told him, he took a small map from his pocket and carefully marked its position. I noticed other markings on the map and asked him what they stood for. He said he had marked the locations of his "temples." I didn't understand. He asked whether I knew why our fellow students had nicknamed him "The Philosopher." I was mystified. He told me to follow him.

We reached one of the city's ethnic museums. He led me in and we walked straight down to the lavatories. They were deserted: it was early afternoon and the whole place was quiet and clean. He turned to me and with a note of pride said: "You can lock yourself in one of these cubicles and not be disturbed for hours! You know how seldom we can get away from meetings. Well, here your privacy is absolute: you can contemplate and enjoy your own world." He proudly displayed his map. "I've discovered more than thirty public buildings in different parts of the city, all with temples like this, all waiting for me."

He began to describe them in meticulous detail. Some of them, especially those built recently, were grandiose: drenched in white marble, with brass and silver trimmings, with florid mosaics on the floor, crystal chandeliers, elaborate systems of ventilation. "You sit in your stall—and think," he continued. "And you hear your thoughts hovering about you like Greek gods suddenly freed from the textbooks. But you are not overheard. What a joy to be left alone at last, not having to care about what others say or how they look at you, or how you seem to them, without having to look outside the white walls of your private sanctuary."

An elderly man approached and went into one of the lavatories. Moments later he left; we listened to the whispers of the exhausted waterfall. "But there is one thing you have to do if you intend to sit inside for any length of time," my friend said. He removed a wad of cotton from his pocket. In it was a small flask of cleaning fluid. "There are all sorts of markings in there," he explained, "messages and slogans scrawled on the walls of the toilets. Many of them clearly the work of counterrevolutionaries. The temples are, apparently, the only place that they can safely discharge their resentment against the regime, against the collective farms, the purge trials and foreign policies, and even against the cult of our omnipotent leader. You see," my friend continued, "I have to be prepared for anyone who accuses me of having scribbled these heresies while sitting in here for a more than normal period. So I begin by wiping off every word on the walls. Then, if I'm asked by a policeman or a detective why I spend so much time in the lavatory, I have a valid and innocent answer. After all, a philosopher once wrote, 'Gods and temples are not easily set up; to establish them rightfully is the work of a mighty intellect.' All of these erasures are a small price to pay for possessing a temple of one's own, don't you think?"

In spite of his fears and apprehensions he faithfully attended all the meetings and seminars. I remember one occasion when the professor asked him to comment upon a political doctrine recently implemented by the Party. He rose, pale and sweating, yet trying to look composed and impersonal; he answered that certain aspects of the doctrine seemed to mirror perfectly the many oppressive aspects of the total state, and for this reason it lacked all humanity. Silence fell. Without comment, the professor gestured for him to sit down. There was a commotion among the students: several Party members got up and noisily left the room. We knew he was doomed.

We continued our studies together until the end of the semester, and then I lost contact with The Philosopher. He had been removed from the university for his antisocial behavior. One of the university officials told me afterward that the man was no longer alive. He almost sneered as he recounted the sordid circumstances of his suicide in a lavatory. I was silent.

●

A spectacular reception was given by the Party for carefully selected local, political, military, and scientific dignitaries and delegates from foreign countries. I was surprised to see among the guests a scientist whom I had met at the university. He was the only living member of a once prominent family which had been exterminated during the purges. After many years spent in a labor camp, he had only recently been rehabilitated by the Party.

After many toasts and speeches the reception

became more casual. The guests left the banquet table, and the waiters moved with difficulty through the crowds, serving drinks from trays they held high above their shoulders. Photographers followed in the steps of the master of ceremonies, who was busy introducing the most prominent guests to each other.

Now the guests began exchanging their national and political badges and insignia, a Party ritual symbolizing mutual understanding.

One guest would approach another, then, bowing, remove a badge from his pocket and pin it to the lapel of his new comrade. I watched the scientist moving through the crowd and pinning onto the chests of the Party functionaries round gold-colored badges, clearly distinguishable next to the highest State medals they wore so proudly. I was just about to leave when I saw him embracing one of the most highly decorated marshals of the country. Leaning toward the marshal's glittering chest, he fastened the golden badge to his uniform, piercing it and the fabric with the pin he held in his right hand.

I approached the marshal for a closer look, and instantly had to restrain myself: the badge was a foreign-made prophylactic. The condom was wrapped and pressed into a shiny golden foil, and the name of the foreign factory stood out clearly in small letters embossed around its edges.

On my way out I saw the results of the scientist's activity: almost all of the high Party and government officials displayed foil-wrapped contraceptives pinned to their lapels. After I left the reception, it occurred to me that only when the dignitaries had reached home and removed their heavy badges would they discover the lighter one. I wondered whether they would remember who had decorated them this way, and if they did, what their reaction would be.

•

The student's union had decided to punish me for my lack of involvement. The Party and the university had approved the recommendation: I was ordered to spend four months as an assistant lecturer in a new agricultural settlement.

It was a long journey, and on the train I shared a compartment with three other men. They were all graduates of economic-planning institutes, eagerly looking forward to their new life, when they were to manage virgin land projects.

The settlement consisted of several collective farms and two experimental breeding stations, linked by a recently completed road. It was managed by a single Party cell. The workers spent six days in the field, using the most modern machines; Sundays were devoted to classroom lectures on social and political subjects.

I realized I would not be accepted. I was eyed with suspicion and was often asked the name of the authority for which I was investigating or spying. My lectures were attended since the schedule required it, but the workers listened to me with hostile politeness or studied disinterest: my requests for questions were met with stony silence. I knew there was no point to what I was doing; it was merely a question of spending the remainder of the four months in the settlement and doing what was required. I hadn't made any friends, and there seemed to be nobody I could consider a companion. In the end I devoted my spare time to studying for my examinations and preparing a report on the lecture series.

During those weeks only one event seemed to excite any general interest. It was the visit of the state circus, which was scheduled to remain at our settlement for several days so that workers from outlying stations could be brought over to see the performances. The program was impressive: there were dancers, clowns, trapeze artists, bareback riders, jugglers, tightrope walkers, and wild-animal acts. The workers, full of admiration for the troupe, constantly broke into exuberant applause, demanding encore after encore.

There was one act I found particularly exciting: a young female acrobat performed with uncanny skill and grace on the trapeze. The girl went through a series of tightrope routines before ending her act with a gymnastic display in which she demonstrated unequaled suppleness. It seemed as though her whole body were molded from a single flexible fiber, so fluid were the complex positions into which she bent herself. Every part of her radiated lightness and strength. As I watched her, I felt turgid and slow.

She climaxed her act by facing the audience,

her legs apart, her hands on her hips, the spotlights playing on her tunic. Then, to an increasingly swift accompaniment from the band, she raised her arms above her head, stood on tiptoe and stretched up and over backward like a taut steel spring. The spotlights followed the perfectly balanced arc of her head as it sank lower and lower; soon only her tightly bound auburn hair reflected the light as her head emerged from between her knees. The entire audience, sensing her suppressed energy, watched with bated breath, expecting her to flick up and back to her original stance. But almost miraculously she coiled her body even more, the lights picking out the gleam of her eyes and teeth as she thrust her head still further forward and up till it shielded her belly. She held this pose for an instant.

The band hit a single, thrilling chord in harmony with the entrancement that had seized everyone, and as the chord struck she seemed to throw her lower limbs forward: her face vanished, and in the second it took us to realize that her head was hidden by her legs, the girl sprang back to her original position, arms up and outthrust as if embracing the applause which filled the air. She stood there, possessed by the tension and energy she had mastered moments earlier. An unwonted desire grew in me.

I watched her performance for three successive nights; the program said she had spent all her life in the circus and had been trained as a trapeze artist and gymnast by her parents, both highly talented performers.

The circus was scheduled to perform for three

/ 74

more evenings; I decided to try to meet the girl. I knew it would be difficult since the circus artists kept to themselves, and I had no convincing reason for intruding upon them. Neither the circus nor the farm managers encouraged any sort of fraternization.

The next day a luncheon was organized for the circus artists and the section leaders of the farm units, so that both groups could toast each other with speeches in praise of their mutual contributions to national life under the leadership of the Party and the government. As the luncheon guests arrived I managed to greet the girl, and immediately led her to a seat at my table. To her left was a wall, and I sat down next to her, beckoning to an elderly farmer to take the seat on my right.

She sat beside me, seemingly oblivious of time and place, looking down at her lap, where she knitted and unknitted her fingers like a paraplegic working through a therapeutic exercise. After a moment she parted her hands and raised them up to her chest. She drew them over her breasts and then down to her hips, thrusting her elbows back, her head and bosom forward.

I looked around the hall. The artists seemed restless, squirming uneasily on the hard wooden chairs. The representatives from the various farm collectives, inured to such meetings, slumped listlessly in their seats. I turned guardedly to the girl.

As I moved she must have moved also, for I felt the pressure of her thigh against mine. I stared across the table at the speaker, affecting great interest. The pressure against me had become a series of slow pushes. I squinted at the girl: she was sitting upright, alternately parting and closing her legs, her knees meeting and whitening with the pressure.

Slowly I placed my hand on the back of her chair, my fingers half clenched and my knuckles extended toward her spine. I couldn't tell whether she noticed or not. As she pulled herself in and back, the material of her dress touched my knuckles. Each of her movements was now more pronounced. I felt as if she were trying to fuse her spine with my knuckles, to make the fleeting contact permanent. Again I looked cautiously at her: her lips tightened and a slight flush heightened the color of her face.

The luncheon ended by midafternoon. The guests left for their dormitories in the clearings along the wooded roadside. The girl and I also left, but we walked quickly into the shelter of the trees.

I told her of the excitement I had experienced in watching her act, describing my fantasy of possessing her at that moment of great tension when her head sprang from between her thighs. She neither paused nor spoke; we walked on.

It was now barely light. No wind reached the lower branches of the birches, and the leaves on the bushes hung inert as though hammered out of lead. Suddenly she turned and stripped, laying her dress down on the leaves piled deep at our feet.

She faced me, gently forcing me down onto my back. As she knelt over me she seemed stocky, almost short-limbed. Her forehead rested on my chest, her hands on the ground behind my shoulders; then, in a single smooth movement, she swung her legs into the air. As they passed the highest point of the arc her back made, they seemed to take on the willowy suppleness of young birch boughs weighed down by falling snow. Her heels slowly passed the crown of her head; with her face framed between her thighs, and her knees bending, she brushed against my face her mouth and womb.

●

No one was able to claim the privilege of being her boy friend; she refused to have a steady companion. Admired, she was never possessed.

At the beginning of the term I was elected editor of the university newspaper. I invited her to contribute a weekly theater column and gave her the freedom to report on any play or literary event that might appeal to her. This post was much sought after and she accepted it immediately.

As editor of the paper I received many invitations and arranged whenever possible for the two of us to attend these gatherings together. I was envied by some of my colleagues, none of whom knew the exact relationship between this girl and myself.

As the term wore on, I noticed her preoccupation with her own body. We would meet at her apartment before going out. From her small living room I often watched her gazing at herself in the dressing-table mirror, examining her profile, craning her neck, drawing her hands over her hips. Her robe, carelessly thrown over her shoulders, was not always closed. Occasionally I ventured a suggestive remark or casually touched her waist while handing her a brush, a dress, or a pair of stockings. She behaved as though she had not noticed anything. After the failure of two or three overtures I acknowledged her restraint.

One day, while she was dressing for a concert, I was sitting a foot or two away from a bureau. The bottom drawer was open, and as I glanced down at some old notebooks and a few odd pieces of costume jewelry I saw a stack of photographs of her, half hidden by the folder in which they lay. I looked toward the bedroom, but she was not at her dressing table. A moment later, when I heard the water running in the bathroom, I leaned over and pulled out a handful of the photographs and slipped them into my inside pocket. After the concert I took the girl home and returned to my own room, where I freely examined them. They showed her nude. The poses, the lighting, the imperfections of focus suggested that she had stood before a camera equipped with a time exposure. They were all fairly recent—the paper had not lost its crispness. I recalled that on several occasions she had stayed after hours in the small office darkroom, saying that she wanted to look over the layouts for the newspaper. Presumably it was then that she had developed the photographs.

I did not mention my discovery to her, nor did I return the photos. Nothing changed in her manner during the next few days, and I assumed she had not noticed the loss.

Whenever I expected a visit from friends, I chose two or three pictures and placed them carefully among my papers and books. I was quite sure that the prints would be examined when I was out of the room preparing drinks or food. Within a few weeks I discovered that those who knew us believed we were lovers, and a few of my closer friends occasionally inquired about our marriage plans.

Shortly before the end of the term the girl and I were invited to a party given at a hotel in a neighboring resort. All of us had been asked to stay overnight and spend the next day swimming. As I had examinations on the following morning, I refused. The girl stayed on, happy enough to be among admirers.

That day, at the end of my exams, I was given a note by the proctor. In answer to the request, I went to the professor's office. He rose when I presented myself, offered me a cigarette, and rather helplessly told me to prepare myself for a shock. The girl had been found dead in the bathroom of the room she had occupied at the hotel: the pilot light of the water heater was on, but not lit.

The next day the news of her death spread through the university. Wherever I went I was stared at or pointed out. Two of my closest friends told me of the prevailing opinion—her death had been a suicide. Later in the day I realized that this conclusion was based more on imagination than on fact, for when I entered the auditorium for the afternoon lecture I found a number of

anonymous notes on my desk. In each one the writer accused me of having seduced the girl, forced her into sexual excesses, photographed her in depraved situations,
and finally of having abandoned her when she became
pregnant.

In the days that followed I was ostracized. I
found myself eating alone in the cafeteria and sitting
without neighbors in the classrooms. On the day of her
funeral almost all of my class attended the service.

At the cemetery the mourners stood around
the grave three-deep, in what would have been a circle
except for the obvious gaps to my immediate right and
left. I felt this sudden isolation even more acutely because my closest friends were standing opposite me, giving me quick, uneasy glances. The grave was open: the
soil was heaped to one side; on the other, the coffin,
flower-decked, rested on the turf. The university chaplain
stood at the head of the coffin, and the girl's parents
waited silently at its foot.

They were probably farmers or small mer-
chants, and I realized suddenly that she had never spoken
to me of her home or family. Covertly I looked at the
man's worn suit, his pale, anguished face. His few wispy
gray hairs blew about in the cold breeze. His wife's legs
bowed grotesquely. It was hard to believe that she and
the worn man beside her had conceived the girl I had
known. Someone bent toward them, whispering. They
raised their heads and looked at me. As they did, all those
present, who had been watching them, now shifted their
gaze to me. Wherever I glanced, I met unyielding stares.
By mistake I looked directly at the father.

For a moment he stared at me. Then he pushed aside his wife, who tripped and had to be stopped from falling by the two gravediggers. Frantically he clawed his way through the crowd. I knew that something violent was about to happen, that the old man would strike me or abuse me. The crowd seemed threatening, like a weight poised to fall at my slightest movement. I could not move.

The crowd gaped. The old man strode on toward me, gasping and puffing, his lips twisted into a lipless grimace. He stopped in front of me, and raising his head with difficulty, spat into my face. I waited. His eyes seemed to sink into their sockets, his hands now fell helplessly at his sides. He turned away, silent, weary, old.

WHEN I WAS *a schoolgirl my parents, the teachers, and our priest always warned me against it.*

You were taught not to do it?

I was taught that if a woman did it, some dreadful punishment, a foul disease or a deformity, would befall her: some of my friends claimed the taste of it was horrible, oily, slimy, lumpy . . . and besides, it was degrading, almost like eating living flesh.

You seem to have thought a lot about it.

/ 82

Yes, often. But I received absolution from the priest.

You went to confession?

Yes; I still go. You see, during confession one doesn't separate the intention from the act; one just confesses one's guilt.

Have you always received absolution?

So far, yes. But just for my thoughts. I'd be embarrassed to say I've actually . . . you know, it's a weird sensation having it in one's mouth. It's as if the entire body of the man, everything, had suddenly shrunk into this one thing. And then it grows and fills the mouth. It becomes forceful, but at the same time remains frail and vulnerable. It could choke me—or I might bite it off. And as it grows, it is I who give it life; my breathing sustains it, and it uncoils like an enormous tongue. I loved what was ejected from you: like hot wax, it was suddenly melting all over me, over my neck and breasts and stomach. I felt as though I were being christened: it was so white and pure.

●

I examined the map but could not identify the road on which I was driving. I decided to take the first turn leading down into the valley, where I would presumably find a small town or at least a sizable village.

Three or four miles farther I was driving past unfenced hayfields on the outskirts of a settlement in which a church overlooked a ragged, dusty square.

Farmhouses and barns stood on the level ground. All was quiet. It was Sunday and there were no signs of life except for the wisps of smoke curling lazily up from a few chimneys. I heard organ music swelling and realized it was the time for midmorning Mass. I stopped the car. I got out, and within seconds dogs were barking and baying on every porch. As I walked forward, their chorus seemed to increase in intensity. Rather than go toward the church, I turned away from the car and found myself approaching a solitary barn standing some yards off the road. I sat down, gazing at the soil which steamed in the sultry heat, at the clover and the unfamiliar wild flowers growing along the fences. The dogs were silent now. The muted voice of the church organ hovered over the houses and barns and lost itself in the fields.

Then I heard a strange sound coming from the barn; I thought it might be the whining of a puppy or the crying of a child. I walked cautiously around the barn, stopping in front of the padlocked doors. I pushed and tugged at the lock, but though it was old, it would not yield. I pulled at it once more: the rotten wood splintered and fell away.

Opening the door I stood on the threshold between light and shadow, listening and peering into the dark interior. Not a sound. As I stepped inside, I could smell dry hay, threshing-floor clay, and moldering wood. For a moment I could see nothing.

Gradually my eyes made out two small plows

with broken handles leaning against a wall along with an old harness and various hoes, rakes, and pitchforks with splayed and crooked tines. In one corner I could see a pile of rusted, burnt-out oven pipes, mounds of scrap, hooks, bent pokers, shovels. Along the other wall stood small buckets filled with nails of many sizes and thicknesses, large metal keys, parts of old irons, broken braziers, sections of window fittings, door handles and locks, pots and pans, pieces of kitchen china. Still further on were rimless wheels, clusters of horseshoes, whips, buckles, and belts hanging on nails, and two axes driven into a short, thick tree stump.

I turned. A startled hen fluttered from under the hay. Flapping her wings and clucking, she picked her way through the half-open door into the barnyard. For a while the stillness was interrupted only by the buzzing of a solitary wasp.

As I was about to walk out, I heard the cry again, which seemed to come from the space under the roof. It was immediately followed by a piercing whine.

I stepped back and opened the door wider, then began to search the dim contour of the rafters. But the daylight did not penetrate. I returned to the car to fetch a flashlight. I entered the barn again.

I focused the flashlight toward the sound. A large cage was suspended from the rafters. Formed of metal grating, it hung down on a heavy rope which passed through a ring secured to the roof. The rope fed down the wall and was fastened to a large cleat.

The strange cry came again: my light beat against the cage. A white hand stretched toward me

/ 85

through the bars; behind it a head, dim but clearly framed in untidy tresses of fair hair, caught the light. I stood undecided, one hand already reaching for the rope. For a second I considered going for help, but I was too curious. I paid out the rope, lowering the cage inch by inch until it swayed just above the floor. Then I secured the line. A naked woman sat behind the grating, babbling meaningless words, staring at me with wide watery eyes.

I approached her. The woman moved, but she did not seem frightened. She stared at me, then began crawling toward me, rubbing her body, scratching and spreading her legs. I noticed her pock-marked face, her gnawed fingernails, her emaciated thighs stippled with bluish bruises. It occurred to me that we were alone in the barn and that she was totally defenseless.

I looked at the woman again: she was obviously demented and now she gestured invitingly, showing her uneven teeth in a twisted smile. I thought there was something very tempting in this situation, where one could become completely oneself with another human being. What I required, however, was the other's recognition of this: the woman in the cage could not acknowledge me.

I hoisted the cage as the woman gibbered through the bars, secured the rope, and left the barn. Outside, I decided not to talk to anyone in the village. An hour later I had reached the district police station.

A sergeant looked on suspiciously as another policeman recorded my account of the woman in the cage. Soon after three police officers drove with me to the village.

We arrived after Mass, just as the streets began to fill with people leaving church. They were dressed in their holiday clothes, the children walking obediently beside the adults. We halted in front of the barn where a tall farmer sat removing his tight boots. One of the policemen asked him some questions and then pushed him into the barn. Our small procession followed them. The festive crowd gathered in silence around our two cars. Then, as if suddenly realizing the purpose of our visit, they scattered to their houses.

Inside the barn, several flashlights converged on the cage, which was now clearly visible. The farmer, sweating and trembling, slowly let down the cage in front of the waiting police; the woman inside was clinging to the grating.

The sergeant snapped out orders to open the lock. The farmer's fingers struggled with the key, but he dared not look at the woman, who cowered afraid in the corner.

The policemen seized her by the legs and arms and dragged her out of the cage. The woman resisted, but they bound her, carried her to the car, and pushed her down onto the rear seat. Then the farmer was handcuffed and thrown in next to his prisoner. I saw the farmer's women staring motionlessly after our departing cars.

Months passed. Finally, after much thought, I decided to return to the village. I left the city at night, so as to arrive at daybreak. I drove slowly, guiding the car carefully over the ruts in the road that wound between the houses. A breeze plucked at the rising mist which covered and then exposed the outlines of the huts and barns. I stopped near the rectory, not entirely sure of my next move. The rectory door slammed and I saw the priest come out. He strode toward the cemetery gateway, disappearing into the heavy shadows cast by the yews which bordered the short path to the church porch. I left the car and hurried after him.

The priest had stopped and was bending over a tombstone, as if trying to trace the vestiges of some inscription eroded by wind and rain. His wrinkled robe was dirty, patched and darned in many places. He started as I came up.

"So you've come all this way just to speak with me . . . why me?" He brushed the wisps of brown moss off his soutane, continuing to look directly at me.

"Because I have something to discuss with you —something important," I said.

"What is your profession?" he asked.

"I'm at the university."

The priest shook some dust out of his sleeve and smoothed his robe. Carefully skirting the graves and stooping to avoid the wet branches, he led me toward the churchyard gate.

In the courtyard of the rectory we were separated by a flock of turkeys pompously crossing our path. The priest waited at the door of the house.

"Would you like a little wine?" he asked.

"Thank you."

We went in. He loosened the sash of his robe and poured out two glasses. We faced each other across the table. "Well, young man, what brings you here?"

"I came because of the cage."

I watched him intently; a flush slowly spread over his puffy face, over the moist folds of his mouth, the pitted cheeks, the eyes deeply set within his creased brow.

"Because . . . ?" he asked.

"The cage," I repeated. "The cage with the woman."

"I can say nothing," he answered. "I only know what you know, that is, as much as the papers have reported." He filled my glass again. "But why are you so concerned?"

"At the moment I'm not. But at the time I was quite concerned. I was the one who found the woman. I was lost, and stopped by the barn."

"So you were the one. Of course, the newspaper report did not name you. Now I remember: the villagers mentioned a stranger who had brought the police." He sipped his wine. "A tragic story. The farmer and his family did not want to pay for hospital care, and so they kept this mad woman in a cage."

"There were some other villagers who knew of the woman—and her prison, Father."

The priest ignored me. "Or for an asylum— the poor creature was unaware of the world she lived in." He set his glass down. "But why return to that affair? The case is closed. The guilty ones have been punished. She's in a hospital now. Have you come here to write another scurrilous article about this scandal? Hasn't enough been said?"

The wrinkled hands emerged from the hollows of his black sleeves; they looked like clusters of scorched weeds as they rested on the sunlit wooden table.

"I have no intention of writing an article, Father: I'm not a reporter. I came back only for the sake of my own conscience, only for myself."

"What do you want, then?"

"I wanted to see you, Father, and talk to you."

"Well, you have seen me, and we have been talking. What else can I do for you?"

"I'm thinking of the years the woman spent in the cage, Father."

"What can I tell you about it that you don't know already?"

"One thing, Father, just one."

"Ask it then and let's be done with it!"

I sipped my wine, watching the broken sunbeams on the rounded bottom of my glass.

"You have lived in the village for over thirty years, Father, including these last five years when scores of men from the village have been doing business in the barn where the woman was. In spite of all their denials the police have proved the men raped and abused her many times. Who could believe all their lies: looking for tools, storing seed, repairing implements, and so on? And the farmer who owned the barn—did he make his money selling cabbages? Even some of the women from the parish knew that the wretched creature had been pregnant twice and that the herb-woman had brought on her miscarriages. These things don't remain a secret long, Father."

"Why are you telling me about it? I read it all in the gazette."

"I'm just thinking out loud, wondering about my own feelings about this matter. It disturbs my peace. Doesn't it disturb yours too, Father?"

"My peace of mind is a matter for my own conscience."

"If, in all these years, not one of the faithful who took part in the many gatherings in the barn has said anything about it to you in the secrecy of the confessional, then, Father, of what value has your stewardship been to this village? Of what value is the religion which you so commend to the people of this community?"

"You have no right, no right whatsoever, to speak of such matters!" His voice picked up an oratorical flourish, but quickly returned to its previous character. He repeated, "You have no right to talk to me about it."

"I do have a right: I opened the cage; I freed that woman. How do you know, Father, that it was not God Himself who led me to the barn that Sunday morning? How well do we know God? I have a right to ask you this, Father, because I can't believe you knew nothing about the caged woman and her tormentors. For thirty years you have been their beloved priest; they spoke of your stewardship with admiration and reverence: of the confessions, the Holy Communions, the absolutions and processions, the liturgy and those saints' anniversaries and holy days so loved by all!

"During the trial I saw their faces, Father, and

they were convinced that the woman in the cage was accursed because of her bastard birth, that she was demented and ill. They argued that she was outside the reach of the Church: after all, she had never even been baptized! Father, I believe that you knew of the cage long before I entered the barn. Why didn't you open the cage and release the woman? This wouldn't have involved revealing confessional secrets; you wouldn't have had to call in the authorities. Why didn't you go to the barn one night while your faithful sinners were asleep and take the woman away? Or were you afraid of the trouble she'd bring being free?"

The priest leaned forward threateningly. It seemed, as the veins of his neck swelled, that his sweat-streaked collar would burst.

"I won't listen!" he shouted. "You understand nothing . . . nothing! You haven't lived in this village for thirty years. What do you know of peasants? I know these people, every one of them. I know them well—they're good fathers, good providers. Sometimes they're weak and they stumble. Yes, I hear their confessions, they bring me their sins like sacrificial offerings; but I also hear them sob as they confess. They don't ask for forgiveness, they implore me, as they would pray for a good harvest. They are my people, and here you come to attack and insult me with preposterous assumptions!"

The priest threw himself back into his chair, ripping off his collar. He was quivering and he tried to control himself. I filled a second glass with wine and slid it across the table to him, watching him as he stared at the enormous painting of a female saint. She was sitting under a palm tree, holding a pair of shears; in front of her, on a platter, lay her severed breasts.

The priest swept his hand toward the wineglass in an awkward gesture of refusal. The glass fell onto the floor, bounced once, and rolled toward the wall. The deep red of the wine, spreading over the table, began to stain the grainy wood. He got up and lurched from the room.

An elderly woman came in. She greeted me shyly and began to wipe off the table with a rag.

I stopped in at the church and sat on one of the benches, where I was soon enveloped in the mossy coolness and the scent of moldering stones. Old women in black were standing and praying in the deeply shadowed nave near the confessional. Now one of them hobbled up to the stall and knelt down, applying first her mouth and then her ear to the wooden grill. When she rose at last, a bony hand thrust out of the darkness of the confessional. The woman leaned over and kissed it; the hand crossed the dank air and withdrew.

Faces peered from the huts as I drove through the village in a cloud of dust. Terrified hens scattered, dogs barked. Soon I reached the main road.

●

The defendant's behavior prejudiced the jury. He never admitted or even seemed to realize that what he had done was a brutal crime; he never argued that he had lost control or had not known what he was doing or that he would never do anything like it again. He just described his encounter with the victim without exaggeration, and in the most ordinary terms.

Almost all of us on the jury were able to discuss and imagine how he had committed the crime and what had impelled him to it. To clarify certain aspects of his case, some of the jurors acted out the role of the accused in an attempt to make the rest of us understand his motives. After the trial, however, I realized that there was very little speculation in the jury room about the victim of the murder. Many of us could easily visualize ourselves in the act of killing, but few of us could project ourselves into the act of being killed in any manner. We did our best to understand the murder: the murderer was a part of our lives; not so the victim.

●

After work I used to rest for a while in a nearby square. Several times I noticed an elegantly dressed man sitting on a bench reading a newspaper. He must have been in his forties and was rather handsome; women often glanced at him, and he would talk with them easily and play with their children. He wore expensive clothes, and sometimes a chauffeur-driven car would arrive to collect him. One day when he was just about to discard an illustrated foreign magazine he had been reading, I approached him and asked if I might have it. We began talking.

Thereafter we met several times, always in the square, where we sat in the shade and watched the passers-by. From the way he looked at and discussed women, it was obvious that he took a keen interest in them. He confided to me that he lived alone and particularly liked associating with show girls from the dance halls and night clubs. For the last twenty years his income was such, he said, that he was in a position to further at one and the same time their careers and his desires.

One day he asked me whether I would like to meet his friends. I instantly agreed. He suggested an intimate gathering of six people at his apartment. We were to be the only men present; the other guests would be show girls. They were not young, he said, but they were willing and experienced. Of course, he added, they wouldn't entertain us spontaneously; he noticed my surprise and quickly explained that nothing mattered as long as it helped bring about someone's fulfillment. This, he said, had been part of his philosophy for a very long time; he had always located the essential truth of his life in his wants and compulsions. He told me to come to his apartment in a week's time.

When I visited him, he led me through a long corridor lined with closed doors. We sat down to a glass of whiskey in the quiet living room, furnished with valuable old-fashioned objects. He saw my curiosity and explained that his guests were already there, each in a separate room off the corridor. He described them briefly and advised me first to join the woman who occupied the room immediately to the left of the living room. After another glass of whiskey we rose; he disappeared without delay into a room on the right side of the corridor, while I stood apprehensively in front of the door he had indicated.

I knocked twice, but there was no answer. I opened the door: the bed covers were turned down; a brightly lit lamp on the night table showed the walls and the ceiling plastered with hundreds of photographs of the same woman, all apparently taken throughout her stage career. No chronology arranged their sequence: some photographs emphasized her young, smooth body, its nakedness exuding sensuality; in others she was heavy and wrinkled, her body, often half clad, spongy and gross. With a single glance I scanned her a hundred times: voluptuously poised on stage, now at ease in the privacy of her room, frozen in every conceivable gesture. Wherever I looked, I met her gaze. As I turned, my attention was attracted by the television set that stood on the table, its screen blank, as though strangely unable to endure an image.

I left the apartment without taking leave of my host. Somewhere in the building a violin was being played. As I walked slowly down the stairs, the music seemed to be chasing the specks of dust that floated in the grayish light.

A few days later I saw the man again. He asked me whether I had enjoyed myself, and he pressed me to return soon to meet his other friends.

•

She never knew I was her lover although we had worked together for a long time in the same office. Our desks were in the same room, and often at lunchtime we sat beside one another in the cafeteria.

It was almost a year now since I had stopped inviting her to dinner or to the theater or to the other functions that she was never willing to attend. I tried to pry some information about her from our fellow workers, but they knew less than I. She had never been close to anyone at the office. One of the men told me he had heard she had been divorced a few years ago, and that her only child was living with its father somewhere in the south.

I began following her. Once I spent an entire Saturday skulking in a doorway across from the building in which she lived. That afternoon she left her apartment and returned at about seven. Before eight she went out again and strolled toward the main thoroughfare. I followed her until she reached the square, where she hailed a taxi. I walked back to my observation post.

Standing in the shallow doorway opposite her house, I waited as the drizzle turned into a persistent rain, drenching my coat. Past midnight a cab stopped in front of the door; she got out alone.

I brooded over my obsession and the absurd vigils it had led me to. Since I seemed to have no chance of becoming her lover, I decided to forge an indirect link through which I could learn more about her. I got hold of one of my friends who I supposed would be able to make contact with her, and confided in him. My friend was prepared for the undertaking, and we immediately began to devise a feasible plan.

He would begin by establishing business dealings between his firm and my employer's. Then he would inquire about certain products that were handled by the department in which the woman worked. Two days later he informed me that he had made a business appointment for the next day and thought it likely he would negotiate directly with her.

As I saw him enter the office I grew tense. Without looking at me, he walked over to the section manager. Then I heard him speaking with the girl.

That afternoon he informed me that all had gone well and a further meeting had been arranged. It was after this second meeting that she accepted his invitation to dinner.

Within the week she became his mistress. He described her as devoted and ready to do anything for him: she had become his instrument, and if I was ready to possess her, he could arrange it. He added that he had already required of her that she submit one day to another man as proof of her love and loyalty to him. He had assured her that she would never know the stranger's identity, because her eyes would be blindfolded. At first she was indignant, claiming she was being humiliated and insulted. Then, he said, she agreed.

The following evening I left my apartment

and took a cab to his house. I arrived too early and had to walk slowly around the neighborhood. Finally I waited silently outside his door, listening. I heard nothing, and rang the bell; the door opened and my friend calmly gestured me in.

A circular white wool rug covered the center of the bedroom floor. A lamp cast its shaded light on the naked woman who lay there, a wide black blindfold covering half her face from the forehead to the base of her nose. My friend knelt down beside her, stroking her with his hands. He beckoned to me. I approached. A melancholy ballad was drifting up from a phonograph; the girl lay still, seemingly unaware of the third presence in the room.

I watched his fingers slide loosely over her skin. As she half rose toward him, seeking him with her hands, he whispered something to her. She dejectedly fell back on the rug, turning her face away from him, her back arched and her hands crossed as though for protection. I hesitated.

Patiently he stroked her again. The cords in her neck softened, her fingers unclenched, but she did not yield any access. My friend rose, and picking up his dressing gown, walked to the door. I heard him turn on the television in the library.

Remembering that I must not speak, I gazed at her tousled hair, her neatly curving thighs, the rounded flesh of her shoulders. I was aware that to her I was no more than a whim of the man she loved, a mere extension of his body, his touch, his love, his contempt. I felt my craving grow as I stood over her, but the consciousness of my role prevailed over my desire to possess her. To overcome this I tried to recall those images of her which had so often aroused me in the office: an underarm glimpsed through the armhole of her sleeveless blouse, the motion of her hips within the confines of her skirt.

I moved closer; she resisted but did not pull away. I began to touch her mouth, her hair, her breasts, her belly, stroking her flesh until she moaned and raised her arms in what could have meant either rejection or appeal. I drew myself up to take her, my eyes closed to shut out her nakedness, my face brushing the smooth blindfold.

I entered her abruptly: she did not resist. With a movement at first timorous and now almost impassioned, her hands gathered me in, pressing my face to her breast. Her loosened hair was spreading around her head, her body tautened, her lips parted in voiceless amazement. Our bodies shuddered; I slid down at her side.

She lay rigid, her hands folded piously on her breast like the medieval effigy of a saint. She was cold and stiff and quiet; only her twisted face had not yet surrendered to the lull which held her body. Her blindfold was stained with the sweat falling from between her drawn brows.

I went to the bathroom, signaling to my host on the way. I dressed and left the apartment. At home I flung myself on the bed. Instantly my image of her divided: the woman in the office, clothed, indifferent, crossing the room; and the naked blindfolded girl, giving herself at another man's command. Both images were clear and sharp—but they refused to merge. For hours each displaced and supplanted the other.

I woke several times during the night, unable to recall the shape or movement of her body, but vividly remembering the smallest details of her clothes. It was as though I were forever undressing her, forever held back by mounds of blouses, skirts, girdles, stockings, coats, and shoes.

Shortly after the war, I remember, I used to catch butterflies. One section of the town had been completely bombed out, and people no longer lived there. Among the ruins, in smelly pits half filled with amorphous objects which had once been utensils, gangs of cats waged war against hordes of starving rats. Here and there, between piles of rotting timber and rubble, among the ashes of gutted houses, weeds and flowers struggled to free themselves from moldy heaps of clay and brick, bursting into sudden stabs of green. Like rebellious shreds of a rainbow, the butterflies swarmed high against the blackened walls. My friends and I would capture them by the dozen in our homemade nets. They were easier to catch than the stray cats, the birds, or even the fierce, hungry rats.

One day we placed some butterflies in a large glass jar and set it upside down, its wide neck overlapping the edge of an old ramshackle table. The gap was wide enough to let in air, but too narrow for the butterflies to escape. We carefully polished the glass. At first, unaware of their confinement, the butterflies tried to fly through the glass. Colliding, they fluttered about like freshly cut flowers which under a magician's hand had suddenly parted from their stems and begun to live a life of their own. But the invisible barrier held them back as though the air had grown rigid around them.

After we had nearly filled the jar with butterflies, we placed lighted matches under the rim. The blue smoke rose slowly about the pulsating blooms inside. At first it seemed that each new match added not death but life to the mass of living petals, for the insects flew faster and faster, colliding with each other, knocking the colored dust off their wings. Each time the smoke dimmed the glass, the butterflies repeated their frantic whirl. We made bets on which of them could battle the smoke the longest, on how many more matches each could survive. The bouquet under the glass grew paler and paler, and when the last of the petals had dropped onto the pile of corpses, we raised the jar to reveal a palette of lifeless wisps. The breeze blew away the smoke—it seemed as if some of the corpses trembled, ready to take wing again.

There was an old abandoned factory on the outskirts of
town. It had been condemned for years; not an unbroken
windowpane remained. There was no equipment left on
any of the floors; even the electric wires had been ripped
out. I slept on the premises without being molested by
anyone. The factory was guarded at night by an old
watchman who did not know I was living there; his
habit of patrolling the yard from nightfall to early morning kept him from entering the buildings. In spite of the
scant attention he gave to anything around him, I found
his presence disturbing.

    The watchman had no place to rest except in a
deep doorway, where he often set his chair and rocked.
I felt that the factory never even entered his mind. It was
quite possible that he was there simply because he had
no better place to go.

    One night, unable to sleep, I watched the old
man move about the yard, stopping every once in a while
to light his pipe. I wondered if it ever occurred to him
that he might not be alone.

    There were a lot of empty beer bottles dis-
carded around the floors, and on the staircase. I quietly
lined up several next to the window, carefully observing
the courtyard and the watchman.

    The first bottle smashed a few steps to the left
of him; he jumped and, shouting, fled into the doorway.

Frightened cats were springing from the empty oil drums. Then all was quiet.

What could he do next? He could remain in the doorway, hidden from my sight, ready to defend himself against further assaults, and wait there until morning. Or he could leave the factory right away. Instead, he emerged and began cautiously veering from side to side as if trying to confuse my aim. Then he bent rapidly to examine the broken glass on the ground. He peered into the shadows around him, possibly still frightened, still conscious of the possibility of a renewed attack, but he could not determine where the bottle had come from. Then he seemed to regain his composure and, relighting his pipe, resumed his rounds.

Again I aimed carefully, letting the second bottle fall right at his feet. Shattering, it muffled his cry. He ran into the doorway, but this time returned just as fast, jerking his head spasmodically.

He obviously would not hide. He must have known that standing in the center of the yard he made a perfect target. When another bottle broke a few feet away from him, he leaped back, but I managed to plant the next one just behind his heels. He scuttled into the shadow of the doorway. There, well hidden, he waited for my next move. Only his pipe glowed in the dark.

What could he have wondered about his enemy? He must have sensed that his life was threatened and that his tormentor was watching from one of the high dark windows overlooking the yard. He knew that he could be killed by one of the bottles.

/ 104

It was dark in the doorway until his match flared up again. Slowly, almost imperceptibly, he began inching along the wall toward the center of the littered area.

I aimed and threw three bottles at once. One of them must have hit his back, for the old man swore loudly, retreating into an alleyway just out of my range. I heard him pacing up and down, angrily thumping the ground with his stick. Unexpectedly he returned into the range of fire. I waited, as he pushed pieces of glass away with his stick and nonchalantly kicked at them while whistling an old cavalry tune.

I fired two bottles at once. The old man did not retreat; he sprang aside with the light steps of a fencer. The next bottles weren't even close; he swung his stick in a mocking salute. I tried again but overshot the mark. By this time the watchman completely ignored the attacks. Only the flickering sparks of his pipe indicated his position. Arranging the remaining bottles as though they were artillery shells, I calculated the distance very carefully.

The next day the newspapers reported that an old man had been hit with a beer bottle thrown by an unknown assailant and had died on the spot. He had become a night watchman when the factory was still in operation and had refused to retire after its closing. Previously he had served a long term in prison for deserting from the army during the war.

●

The taxi moved quickly through the streets of the capital, past the Party buildings, the university with its historical statues, the museums and modern skyscrapers, then across the bridge over the river. I was on my way to the airport. I realized what I now saw I was seeing for the last time.

Scattered somewhere around those buildings, suspended between those monuments like wisps, were twenty-four years of my life. The knowledge brought me no emotion: it could have been twenty-four days or twenty-four centuries. My memory, broken and uneven, was like an old cobblestone road.

The airport. Passport control. The plush seat on the plane. The takeoff. I continued to reflect that my own quarter of this century had been spent waiting for this departure, that the time into which I was now entering was inconceivable. Now, airborne, I grew uneasy that I had done nothing in the last years to make my imminent arrival in another continent more real. Only the departure had reality. I felt cheated and robbed: so many years had led to nothing more than a seat on a plane.

Had it been possible for me to fix the plane permanently in the sky, to defy the winds and clouds and all the forces pushing it upward and pulling it earthward, I would have willingly done so. I would have stayed in my seat with my eyes closed, all strength and passion gone, my mind as quiescent as a coat rack under a forgotten hat, and I would have remained there, timeless, unmeasured, unjudged, bothering no one, suspended forever between my past and my future.

THE PLANE LANDED and rolled to its final stop in front of the terminal building. I put on my fur overcoat. Though it was winter, a warm springlike rain continued to fall.

It was a splendid coat, made of Siberian wolf fur, soft and silvery, with an enormous collar and great flapping sleeves. I had bought it in a small town in the middle of the steppes. I remembered the man who sold it to me had tried to convince me that only in such a coat could one dare to cross the North Pole, that only in the Western countries could one afford such a coat.

The walk between the aircraft and the buildings was out of doors; with every step my coat became heavier, more and more rain-sodden.

I walked through the long corridor to the customs control, leaving behind me a trail of water. The other passengers stared at me curiously. No one else was wearing a fur coat, and it occurred to me that the salesman of the steppes had considerably exaggerated the riches of the West. I collected my suitcase, which was loaded with dictionaries, and was about to cross the main waiting room when the handle suddenly tore loose and the suitcase hit the floor, bursting apart like a gigantic clamshell, spewing out its contents. People jerked their heads, children laughed.

The youth hostel was filled. The manager, after I had bribed him with several rolls of film, allowed me to sleep in a windowless workshop adjoining the boiler room. In the evening, when automatic devices had started the boiler, hot water began to surge through the pipes and walls, filling the air with radiant heat. My fur, still heavy from the day's rain, steamed as though pressed with an iron. First the collar dried, then the shoulders, the back, and finally the cuffs and front. With the last bit of dampness gone, the coat shrank and grew stiff, its pelt roughened by the bunches of hair knotted and stuck to each other. Almost simultaneously there seemed to be no air left in the room. My mouth and nose were parched; I tossed from side to side on my pallet.

Each morning I hoped that snow and frost

would come to save my coat from dying, to breathe new life into its sagging shoulders, to stretch its sleeves and spread fresh luster over the once gleaming back.

I had no other coat to wear when I went out looking for work. It rained for the next few days: the fur was slowly turning into a matted lump.

I spent the day offering my services in the neighborhood, but since I hardly spoke the language, I received no offers. My last roll of film had gone for a meal. I walked about the streets, more and more aware of my fascination for the shop windows full of food. I was famished.

There was an abundance of food in all the shops and supermarkets, but none was crowded enough to absorb a hungry thief in a fur coat. In addition to the salespeople, there were panoramic mirrors hung strategically under the ceilings, in which I saw myself grotesquely enlarged or flattened like a griddle against a background of exotic fruits. I was strongly inclined to steal an apple or a roll but was never brave enough to do so. I gave up and left the stores, stared at by amused shoppers.

More people crowded the shops in the evening. I was growing both hungrier and bolder. I wandered about a large supermarket, sniffing its odors, trying not to brush against the other customers with my wet coat, constantly on the lookout for some nutritional food small enough to conceal. It occurred to me that the small jars in front of me could be hidden in the palm of my hand and then dropped quickly into the upper front pocket of my coat. I fingered one of the cold objects for a moment, lifted my hand to my chin, then allowed it to escape through my bent fingers directly into my pocket. I left the shop in cool composure. In the days that followed I visited many stores. Aware of its value as a restorative, I stole only black caviar.

●

I was recruited to chip the paint and rust from a ship scheduled for refitting. The recruiter said that the work had to be done during the night since it was illegal for non-union men to work on the ship. He explained that there were never complaints from the union as long as the less demanding, better-paid painting jobs went to its work crews. The painting could not be started until the old layers had been removed, and paint scraping was far beneath the dignity of union men when better jobs were to be had.

At night we were taken in large gangs to the ship. The recruits were always newly arrived immigrants, always poor, often destitute. Many of them had entered the country illegally or had other reasons for avoiding the authorities. The pay was one third of the going rate, but I was relieved to have some money coming in regularly.

Though the ship was moored at the quay, she rolled as choppy winter currents pulled at her. We were given neither boots nor coveralls—just handed broad-faced chisels and hammers. We had to chip the paint so as not to let flakes fall on our fellow workers. As I worked, the scraps flew off into my face and clothing.

Poised in our slings, we dangled high above the water, swaying as icy winds blew in from the sea. The ship's portholes were dark; every time I peered into one of them I longed to be inside the cabin that lay behind. I longed to be the only passenger on that deserted ship, protected all about by steel walls, able to sleep and then awaken to some faraway sea, my identity gone, my destination uncharted.

I worked wearing my fur coat, which soon became flecked with gummy particles of paint, growing stiffer and heavier by the hour. In the early morning I returned to my overheated room. The heat mingling with the smell of paint left me weak and nauseated. I picked at the paint flakes before sleeping, hoping to get them off the coat before they hardened. But I was always too exhausted, and there was never enough time.

Later in the day, when I wanted to go out, I met with further opposition from my coat. Its sleeves resisted the entrance of my arms, its pockets seemed sealed against my hands. As I closed the coat across my chest, the front creaked in protest.

The recruiter asked me to deliver an envelope to one of my fellow workers. The name and address were written in foreign characters. I didn't know the language, but I knew its alphabet and could read single words. I went up on deck to call out the name, trying to pronounce it correctly.

A man came over to claim the envelope,

speaking in a foreign language. I gestured that I did not understand. He spoke again. I did not know what he said. He left, returning a few minutes later with three men; speaking excitedly, they surrounded me. I tried to show them that I could not understand them, but they would not believe me. I realized that they thought I was one of them but ashamed of admitting it.

I was jostled by them. Although the coat protected my body from their blows, I was afraid I would be shoved overboard and that my heavy coat would drown me. I saw myself on the sea bed, my coat covering me like a shroud. As they continued pummeling me, the buttons popped, the coat split along the seams. At this moment the recruiter appeared and my attackers held back. I rose, clutching the tattered fur strips to myself. The recruiter called me a troublemaker: I had to leave the ship immediately and stay away.

●

I worked in a long, narrow parking lot and lived off the tips I received. One day a man returned for his luxurious foreign car. When I brought it up, he asked me about the country of my origin. Then he motioned me to get into the car next to him and inquired directly whether I would like to make some money. He showed me a roll of bills, saying that if I were smart, I could earn this kind of money, enough to buy a car like his and have enough left over to keep a girl for a week in the best hotel in the city.

After questioning me about my life, he said he too had once been a newcomer to this country. Most people here knew where the money was, but they didn't know how to get their share. A few, like himself, had more than their share. He added that in today's world it was hard to spend a lot of money unless you could account for its source to the tax people. There had to be a legitimate business, he emphasized, through which the money could be passed so it would look clean.

He pulled a banknote from his pocket; it was enough to support me for three months. He tore it in two and gave me one half, telling me I could have the other half if I delivered a message. He told me there was a restaurant near the parking lot, owned by an old man with two daughters. The place, though quite large, had very few customers. The old man had been approached several times by people, each of them interested either in acquiring his restaurant or in becoming his partner. But he wouldn't accept any offers.

Since the old man had originally come from the same country as I had, my prospective employer was hoping that his offer would carry more weight if I conveyed it. He thought I looked very persuasive. The message was simply to ask the old man to enter into a partnership with a cousin of my new acquaintance. The old man, if he agreed, would get a comfortable cut of the profits. He had only to call the phone number I would give him and everything would be arranged. If he refused, I would tell him he had no choice—if he loved his daughters. I realized immediately that the purpose of such a partnership was to make the restaurant appear more profitable than it actually was, thus allowing illegally gained money to be passed through the books.

I went to see the old man. In the restaurant there was only a woman mopping the floor, and I told her I wished to see the owner. She called him. When I greeted him, he immediately recognized my accent and remarked that we must have come from the same region.

First I told him I had a message from someone trying to help him. He said he didn't need any help from strangers. During the last war his paralyzed wife had been helped onto a train headed for a concentration camp. Those who helped her were young and willing and neatly uniformed, he said. He didn't want any help from strangers, he repeated. Then, as instructed, I asked about his daughters. His lips grew white. "Why do you speak of my children?" he asked. "They have nothing to do with my business. How do you know about them?"

"The man who sent me doesn't distinguish between your family and your business," I said. "He told me about your daughters: your younger one walks to school every morning, and the older crosses the avenue for her piano lessons. He even knows who their dentist is."

The old man stood up, trembling. "I'm going to call the police!" he shouted, but did not move from the table.

"You won't," I said. "The police are young

and willing and neatly uniformed. Do you think they are going to walk your daughters to school, to the dentist, to the music teacher every day? Tell me," I asked. He sat still, burying his face in his hands.

"The man who sent me here," I said, "loves music too. He told me it would be a great pity if your daughter should hurt her hands and never become a concert pianist. The man who sent me also said that an old man who has lost all his relatives shouldn't place a restaurant above his children."

The old man was silent. As I waited I heard a piano upstairs. He noticed my attention. "She will become a great pianist one day," he said. "To her, music means more than words." He reflected: "Give me the man's telephone number. I'll call him. I have to have that partner."

The next morning, as usual, I was at the parking lot. At noon my new employer drove up. "You did a good job," he said. "One day you may become a lawyer or a restaurant owner yourself." Between his fingers he held the remaining half of the banknote.

About a year later I went to see my favorite barber. He had recently arrived in this country, taken over a small shop, and started his own business. It was a bright, clean shop, and one could see right into it through the large street window. My barber seemed tense and upset; he didn't want to shave me, he said, because he was too nervous. I suspected something must be seriously wrong and suggested we go to a café together and talk.

At lunch the barber told me what had happened. A few days before, a visitor had brought him a message—his shop window needed protection. If he refused to pay, it would be smashed up by neighborhood hoodlums. The barber said that he had been in business for over a year and that there had never been any trouble —why would they want to break his window now? In any case, he had insurance which would pay for the breakage. But the visitor insisted he knew some young men who rode around at night on motorcycles heaving bricks through the windows of certain establishments; of course, even the most generous insurance company wouldn't keep on paying for smashed windows; besides, repairing the damage slowed up business. Therefore, the barber's visitor suggested he should subscribe to the unofficial neighborhood protection service, as many other small businesses had already done. The monthly fee was based on the assessment of the business turnover. His protection would cost more than half his net income. He had a week to make up his mind.

"What do you intend to do?" I asked.

"I can't pay. I've got a pregnant wife. I know the police can't protect me for long. I'm bound to lose. I'll have to sell my shop."

I saw at once that the barber didn't know how to fight. I told him that I could settle the matter if he made me his partner. At first he didn't believe me, but I explained further. Then I took him to the bank and to a lawyer's office to have the partnership deeds drawn up. By the end of the day I was his legal partner. At the end of the week my partner referred the protection man to me.

He introduced himself on the telephone.

When I asked where he was calling from, he said he was in his car in front of my apartment building. I looked out the window: a man with a telephone receiver in one hand waved to me from a sports car. I returned to the phone and invited him up. He came.

"Do you like my car?" he asked. "It's a beauty, isn't it?"

I told him I admired the car.

"It gives you a great feeling of power," he said. "You get in with a beautiful woman alongside you and start the engine; when you let out the clutch the car moves forward so rapidly that if you have your hand on the girl's knee, she will feel you way up inside her."

He looked around, sat down, and pushed aside the books on the table. "What are all the books for? I thought you trimmed the outside of people's heads?"

I answered that barbering was only a recent hobby of mine, just as sports cars was probably a new one of his. I asked what he wanted, and he repeated what he had told the barber the week before. I informed him that I had no intention of paying for protection and expected the window of my barber shop to remain intact.

With my visitor still present, I rang up the man who had used my services in the matter of the restaurant. I recognized his voice at once when he answered the phone, but I had to remind him when and how we had met. I told him I was now in business, that I had not become a lawyer or even a restaurant owner, as he had once suggested, but simply a partner in a small barber shop that was being threatened. I asked him to help me as I had once helped him. I didn't know whether he was in touch with those who forced protection on barber shops, I said, but I had great trust in his power and connections. If he did not wish to help me, I added, and if my shop window should be smashed, I would do to him, or his cousin, or their families, what he had once planned to do to the daughters of the old restaurant keeper. I had no children or family myself, I continued, but I had been a sniper in the army. I knew the city well, and though I might eventually lose out, I intended to be a very costly victim.

I did not wait for his comment but motioned my visitor to the phone. Somewhat confused, he took the receiver. The two men talked for a while in a foreign language. I don't know what they said, but the man left a minute later without a word.

I saw my partner the next day and told him what had happened. He was still upset and frightened. Weeks passed. Some store windows nearby were smashed, but ours remained untouched. After a while we quietly dissolved our partnership.

●

He played drums in the small band which was the neighborhood restaurant's chief attraction. I went there often, and he must have noticed me sitting alone, because one evening, in the interval between sets, he came over and asked if he could talk to me. He said he had heard I was looking for a job, and he had something to offer me. He explained that playing the drums was only a hobby and that during the day he worked as a truck driver. After playing the drums all night, he went on, he was too tired to drive the truck alertly. He did not want to lose his well-paying steady job as a driver, but he also wanted to remain in the band. He asked me if I would occasionally drive for him. He said he would pay me well.

He picked me up early the next morning to teach me to drive the truck. It was enormous, with a six-wheel cabin detached from a trailer riding on four sets of wheels. When I swung the truck into a turn, the trailer resisted as if with a life of its own, holding relentlessly to its own path like the stiffened body of a huge snake. Learning to drive the truck took up the entire weekend.

Monday I was on my own. The truck depot was on the outskirts of the city. It had its own shifting population of mechanics, loaders, dispatchers, and drivers. I went directly to the truck, checked the tires and brakes, warmed up the engine, and after looking over my route maps, drove from the depot into the streets.

I was to transport hats from a factory to shops spread throughout the city. I was terrified not only by the size of the vehicle but by avenues which were suddenly off-limits to commercial traffic, streets that became too narrow or too congested for me to pass through, temporarily closed squares, children, construction sites, everything.

Each time I stopped to check my map or ask

directions, the traffic behind me also stopped; any attempt to back up could stall traffic for miles and bring a police patrol.

I drove the truck through the dense streets, my attention shifting from what lay ahead to what was happening in the rear. I had to assess distances in advance and compute the space available for the turn of the cabin and the wide arc of the trailer. I could trust no one—certainly not the foreshortened views of strollers I had in the side mirrors, not the passers-by who crossed the streets or stepped down from the sidewalks directly in front of my truck.

Of necessity the truck and I became one. I began to feel with my body the space between the rear tires and the edge of the sidewalk and the space between the truck and precariously parked bicycles. I knew which wheel would flatten an empty beer can, and I could gauge the inch left between the clearance batons on the front fender and the uniform of a policeman directing traffic. I discovered that driving the truck had something in common with what I had experienced on skis. I had to project myself beyond my body into a motion that had not yet begun but was imminent and irreversible.

One morning while driving through the business district, I noticed a car steadily following the trailer. I was afraid I was being tailed by the police or by a union official. As I slowed down, the car passed and the Negro driver signaled me to stop. When I parked, he came over and told me he liked the way I drove: he was impressed by my confidence, speed, and good control. He would like me, he said, to become his chauffeur and was willing to double my current wages. I looked at his guileless face and at the soft interior of his car.

All he wanted me to do, he continued, was to drive his car as fast and as skillfully as I drove my truck. But he had another reason for hiring me. He explained that it was not because I was white and he black. It was rather because he and his associates met regularly in the car to discuss important business. The car had to be kept in motion during these meetings to preclude others, whom he referred to as "the other guys," from eavesdropping. He explained that his business was of a nature that no outsider should try to understand. Not only did he want me to keep the car moving during these meetings, but also to drive it at high speed and keep it very close to other cars, giving his associates the impression that a collision was imminent. This, he hoped, would frighten them into paying far less attention to him than usual. It was certain, he argued, that their pride would not allow them to show their fear to a white man.

I accepted his offer. The car was beautifully responsive, and I quickly became accustomed to its power and comfort. As I drove around the city with my new employer, he would comment on my driving, encouraging me to drive faster and to take even more risks in passing the other cars.

After hours of practice, my speed and the closeness of my passing maneuver no longer drew criticism from my employer. Several times he even lost his composure, throwing up his hands as if to protect himself from a certain crash. He could not believe the car emerged unscathed.

One morning we collected his associates. After they had seated themselves in the rear, my employer gave me directions and the order to start.

I drove off at high speed. The passengers braced themselves against the front seat and stared with incredulous horror through the windows. My employer sat next to me, relaxed and half facing the others, nonchalantly resting his arm on the dashboard. Then the discussion between them began. Judging by the sudden interruptions and the long pauses, his guests were too astonished by their predicament to concentrate on business. I expected to be asked to slow down or instructed to drive with greater care, but each time I looked into the rearview mirror I caught grimaces of affected calm.

When the conference ended, my employer ordered me to stop the car. I got out and opened the door. The passengers emerged, perspiring and shaken. None of them looked at me.

●

He said he was sure I could win money, and went on to explain the sport involved. It was called "book-knock-off." The requirements of the competition were simple: the drivers had to agree upon the course for the contest.

Usually a one-way street was selected, with cars parked either on one or on both sides. Referees would tape books selected for their weight to the sides of the cars parked on the appointed street. They were about two or three inches thick, and fixed at bumper height; none of the drivers knew in advance on which cars the books were taped. Then the drivers, waiting in their cars two blocks from the course, would be waved in one by one by the referee. When signaled, a driver had to drive over the course at a minimum speed of fifty miles an hour and keep close enough to the cars with books taped to them for the bumper of his own car to dislodge as many of them as possible.

The timekeeper clocked each driver, and the referee counted the dislodged books. The driver who knocked off the greatest number of books was declared the winner.

A cash prize was contributed by the owners of the competing cars. This, together with the sums collected from bets, was split between the winning driver and the owner of the car.

My employer told me that he had enough confidence in my skill to sponsor me as the driver of his new and costly car. He was certain that his car would attract heavier bets against it, since the driver would be expected to perform more cautiously in order to avoid damaging so high-priced a vehicle. He guaranteed me the usual one third of the stake, but warned that if I lost three times, he would no longer sponsor me.

The speed of the cars and the damage they caused made the races illegal. They took place surreptitiously at night on poorly lit streets that had little traffic and were rarely patrolled.

Arriving with my employer for our first competition, I found the street filled with spectators. The referee and his helpers had already taped books to cars parked bumper to bumper along the street.

The assembled drivers were shaking hands with each other and with the referee. The spectators examined the cars we were about to drive and placed their final bets. The referee flipped a coin to decide on which side of the street each driver would make his run. It fell to me to drive on the right-hand side of the street, the side farthest from my line of vision.

The first driver took off; I could hear the screech of tires and the thud of the books as his car sent them careering onto the street. The referee counted the books, and the helpers replaced them on different cars. Then my turn came.

My headlights were reflected in the shiny bumpers of the parked cars. I could not see the books from behind the steering wheel, but I knew they were there, waiting motionless to be prized off like limpets, their crumpled pages bound tightly between the stiff leather of the gilt bindings. I raced into the final stretch, bearing hard to the right, staring into the beam of my headlight to catch even the slightest glimpse of my targets, straining to hear the books falling, and bracing myself against the half-expected shriek of steel on steel. I was guided by instinct rather than sight. Having completed my run, I was eager to learn the result, and walked over to the referee. My speed had been equal to that of the other competitors, but I had knocked off twice as many books. My employer ran over and embraced me excitedly. Together we collected the prize money; he paid me my share at once.

The second group of drivers was now ready to compete. As the winner of the first round, I could race again. The referee spun a coin. Again I drew the right-hand side as my course. The first driver began his run. Moments later we heard the sharp crack of contact: the man had held too tight a course and his fender had hit a parked car; his slowing-down lost him the race. My turn came again.

I recalled a man who had lost his arms during the war. He claimed that despite his loss he had not ceased to feel his hands and fingertips; he said it was as if his absent limbs had become organs sensing through echoes, which had the effect of extending the other parts of his body to objects and places they could not otherwise reach. I too felt such echoes.

I slipped a stereo tape into the car's player, and as the music heightened my tension, I accelerated; my nerves gauged the steering, the speed, and the distance. I sensed I was knocking off one book after another. I won.

Weeks passed. The game continued in different areas of the city. I became well known and raced against many drivers, never losing to any of them. One night these games came to an end.

There was a couple in one of the parked cars along the course. The roar of the passing cars and the angry revving of the engines must have disturbed them. Suddenly one threw open the car door and got out, standing there amazed, shielded momentarily by the door. In that instant a competing car rammed into the door, slamming it closed. The body disappeared. Only the head remained outside, as if balanced on the knife-edge of the door; then it rolled down and hit the asphalt like one more book that had been struck off.

The crowd and the drivers panicked and dispersed. In the days that followed there was an intensive police investigation.

●

How did you meet her?

She lived in my building.

Then it was by accident?

Not exactly. There were several hundred tenants in the building—it's a whole city block long, you know—and I had listened in to the voices of a considerable number of them. Her voice was among the voices.

What do you mean "among their voices"?

I mean their voices; you see, I signed my lease when the building was still under construction, and I was able to wander around the unfinished apartments. At that time I was interested in electronics. In all the apartments on my floor and on the two floors directly beneath, I concealed a miniature microphone, which also acted as a transmitter. The device was no larger than a button, yet it picked up every sound and could transmit a signal for a quarter of a mile. I installed a specially designed radio in my apartment with which I could receive transmissions at any time I chose—and so I listened to their voices.

But that's incredible! How did you get those microphones?

The same way everybody else does—they're advertised in magazines and sold by mail-order.

How long did you listen to those voices, those people?

For months. Of course, at first I had difficulty identifying the voices. On my radio I could monitor one voice at a time, but I was not able to pinpoint the apartment it came from. I had to be very careful. For instance, I could not walk around the corridors for too long, waiting to see who came out of the apartments where I had hidden microphones. In trying to identify those I suspected, I had to be very casual—starting conversations in the elevators and greeting people in the hallways. I spent almost three months attempting to match the voices with the people I supposed I had been listening to.

But—were you able to do this?

Yes. I've identified all of them. But, of course, very few really interested me.

I suppose that woman did.

Yes. She had an apartment on my floor. I recognized her voice when she was greeting someone in the lobby. She was among those I had been listening to for a long time.

What did you do?

I stayed at home for several days and moni-tored her apartment. She lived alone, and she didn't work. I could listen to her all morning when the "other voices" were away.

How did you manage to meet her?

I started collecting signatures for a complaint about the untidy corridors and the faulty air condition-ing. I called on her among the other tenants. Then I began to date her.

Wasn't that unfair? I mean, you had such an advantage over her.

To a degree, yes, I did have an advantage. But before I actually met her, there was still a lot I didn't know about her life. For example, there had often been long silences in her apartment; I had heard noises I could not identify: even what I recognized as her voice would suddenly change as if purposely controlled. At other times there were whispers and conversations which were sometimes drowned out by the radio, the record player, or the television.

After you began dating her—did you tell her that you had been listening in on her?

No.

Did you still go on listening to her apartment?

For a while I did. But I soon stopped. I felt like a scientist who has completed his study: the speci-men he has observed and recorded and analyzed for such a long time has ceased to be a mystery. Now I could ma-nipulate her: she was in love with me.

It occurred to me then that if I introduced her to drugs of a certain kind, and if she became addicted, she might free herself from what she had been. She might emerge as a very different woman, and though I retained possession of her, my knowledge of what she had been would have no more value. A new relationship would begin.

Her addiction might regenerate all that had become flabby and moribund in her and at the same time break down what was stiff and rigid; she would acquire new desires and new habits and liberate herself from what she thought of me, from what she felt for me. Like a polyp she would expand and develop in unpredictable directions.

●

When you are inside me, why do you urge me to caress myself at the same time? I feel you, so why must I touch myself?

You admitted my love-making forces you to become more aware of your body.

It does, but doing that to myself: it seems perverse.

Surely it stimulates you and excites you more?
Yes, it does.
Then simply give yourself up to what you

feel: enjoy that awareness. Lovers are not snails; they don't have to protrude from their shells and meet each other halfway. Meet me within your own self.

I never thought of it as you see it; that would not come naturally to me. But you, what do you feel?

I want you, you alone. But beyond you and me together, I see myself in our love-making. It is this vision of myself as your lover I wish to retain and make more real.

But you do want me for what I am, apart from you, don't you?

I don't know you apart from myself. When I am alone, when you are not here, you are no longer real: then, it's only imagining again.

Then, all you need me for is to provide a stage on which you can project and view yourself, and see how your discarded experiences become alive again when they affect me. Am I right? You don't want me to love you; all you want is for me to abandon myself to the dreams and fantasies which you inspire in me. All you want is to prolong this impulse, this moment.

●

You were asleep, you did not hear the bell.
Who was it?
The dealer, bringing the drugs.

Oh, yes. The rich one. Is he making a lot of money?

He's making money now.

What do you mean?

He began as a delivery boy, working for a neighborhood pharmacist. He used to pick up the prescriptions from steady customers and then deliver the drugs to them. One day he was approached by a well-dressed, successful older man who asked him whether he would like to make more money—four or five times more than he was making then. The boy said he wanted to.

All the older man asked him to do was copy down the names of the customers who repeatedly ordered certain drugs and who became irritable or angry when delivery was delayed.

●

I walked through the districts where they lived surrounded by fetor and disease. They had nothing to possess or to be proud of. They were united only by the shade of their skin—and I envied them.

I walked the streets in the heat of the sultry day and peered into rooms full of screaming infants and rotten mattresses piled on the floor, the old and the sick lying flattened on their beds or bending low in their chairs. In the dead-end alleys I watched the girls in groups, giggling. I stared at the shouting boys playing ball in the empty lots, saw the paralyzed and the doped sprawled on the sidewalks—living obstacles for the blind and the half-witted. I watched the dirt-smeared children smashing bottles against the never-emptied garbage cans, chasing cats and dogs and each other around the abandoned cars from which everything of value and every shred of rubber and fabric had been stripped by persistent petty thieves.

I envied those who lived here and seemed so free, having nothing to regret and nothing to look forward to. In the world of birth certificates, medical examinations, punch cards and computers, in the world of telephone books, passports, bank accounts, insurance plans, wills, credit cards, pensions, mortgages, and loans they lived unattached, each of them aware only of himself.

If I could magically speak their language and change the shade of my skin, the shape of my skull, the texture of my hair, I would transform myself into one of them. This way I would drive away from me the image of what I once had been and what I might become; would drive away the fear of the law which I had learned, the idea of what failure meant, the yardstick of success; would banish the dream of possession, of things to be owned, used, and consumed, and the symbols of ownership—credentials, diplomas, deeds. This change would give me no other choice but to remain alive.

Thus the world would begin and die with me. I would see the city as a mutant among the wonders of the world, its chimneys polluting the air, its roots poisoning the earth, its tentacles setting one man against another and strangling them both in their hopeless contest. I would map the city's highways and tunnels and bridges, its subways and canals, its neighborhoods adorned by beautiful homes filled with priceless objects, rare libraries, and fine rooms, its clever networks of pipes and cables and wires under the streets, its police departments and communications stations, its hospitals, churches, and temples, its administrative buildings crowded with overworked computers, telephones, and servile clerks. Then I would wage war against this city as if it were a living body.

I would welcome the night, sister of my skin, cousin of my shadow, and have her shelter me and help me in my battle. I would lift the steel lids from the gutters and drop explosives into the black pits. And then I would run away and hide, waiting for the thunder which would trap in mute telephone wires millions of unheard words, which would darken rooms full of white light and fearful people.

I would wait for the midnight storm which whips the streets and blurs all shapes, and I would hold my knife against the back of a doorman, yawning in his gold-frogged uniform, and force him to lead me up the stairs, where I would plunge my knife into his body. I would visit the rich and the comfortable and the unaware, and their last screams would suffocate in their ornate curtains, old tapestries, and priceless carpets. Their dead bodies, pinned down by broken statues, would be gazed upon by slashed family portraits.

Then I would run to the highways and speedways that surge forward toward the city. I would have with me bags full of bent nails to empty on their asphalt. I would wait for the dawn to see cars, trucks, buses approaching at great speed, and hear the bursting of their tires, the screech of their wheels, the thunder of their steel bodies—suddenly grown weak as they crashed into each other like wineglasses pushed off the table.

And in the morning I would go to sleep, smiling in the face of the day, the brother of my enemy.

IF I COULD *become one of them, if I could only part with my language, my manner, my belongings.*

•

I was in a bar in a run-down section of the city beyond the covered bazaar. Without hesitating I walked over to the

/ 136

bartender. As he leaned forward I began my deaf-mute charade, signaling for a glass of water. The barman waved me away impatiently, but I stood my ground and repeated my pantomime. I could feel the stares of the people in the bar. When I jerked my shoulders and flapped my ear like a spastic they scrutinized me closely, and I sensed that to some of them I had suddenly become an object of interest. I knew I had to be very careful of their suspicions, of any attempt to find out who I was or where I had come from.

Two men and a woman edged nearer, and touched me. At first I ignored their overtures, giving the woman, the boldest and most silent, a chance to elbow the others aside.

I continued to motion for water. A man came forward to order a drink for me, but I refused, grimacing my disgust for arrack and gesturing apologies for my refusal. A couple drew closer. They beckoned me to leave with them. I did not understand what they were saying, and making a show of being attracted to the bright jewelry they wore, I turned and slowly looked into their faces. Their gaze bore down on me.

There was a store I entered several times. Nothing distinguished it from the others of the neighborhood. Most of the shops and bars in the vicinity had some connection with illegal activities—the black-market, stolen goods, or traffic in young country girls. Often I hung around the shop until closing time, and watched the patrons wandering out the back door to the barn in the yard. As a silent, gesturing spastic I was not a threat to the callers—I could be given a task, a few coins, and then be dismissed. Eventually I followed them, but was pushed back into the shop and out into the street. The final time I stayed late and tried to join the men. No one stopped me, but at the barn door a woman motioned me to stand guard.

From my vantage point I peered into the barn. I saw a great circle of naked men lying on their backs, their feet joined at the center like the spokes of a wheel. A woman was standing at their feet, pulling off her ragged dress. She was gross and heavy, her skin moist and hairy. She was splashing water from a wooden bucket over her belly and legs. And as she washed herself and the water spattered on the ground, the men fidgeted, their hands playing at their thighs or their arms shifting behind their heads. It was as though she had become the healer of these broken men, and at the sound of the water a momentary surge went through these petty thieves and weary pimps. She plodded across to one of them, squatting over him. For a moment he grunted, cried out hoarsely, half rose, and then fell heavily back. The woman stepped away from him and passed on to his neighbor, picking her way like a bloated toad over the worn stones of a mudhole. One by one she served them; those she had not yet reached twitched in their efforts to restrain the energy that surged through their loins. One by one they fell back, like corpses laid out in shallow coffins. Now the barn looked as if it had been pressed into service for the dead and the dying from a derailed train. As she rose and walked around the silent men, the woman resembled a nurse checking the victims. She bathed, and again the water splashed. Now there was no answering sound, no movement.

At times my disguise became a hazard. One day, wandering about longer than usual, I decided to have a meal before finding a place to sleep. I went into a place that I knew was usually crowded. The bar itself was almost empty that night. But I spotted several familiar faces—a group of manual workers in the front of the room and two or three of the local bosses, their heads together, at the private tables in the back.

A surly peasant stood at the counter, mumbling as he drank. Away by the wall, half lost in the shadows, a man was slumped over his glass.

Suddenly the street door blew open and a dozen policemen rushed in. Some stationed themselves between the door and the crowd; others followed a kitchen boy to the man drooping at the bar.

The police first sat the man up, then pulled him off the stool. As his body swung around I caught sight of the knife that stuck out from his ribs. There was a bloodstain on the wall. The crowd broke into a frenzy of talk. Only then did I realize that I was the likeliest suspect of them all. There could be no explanation for my dress, my acts, or my presence.

If I continued to be a deaf-mute, I would be accused of this crime, the senseless act of a defective. My mask would trap me further. But if I were to bolt through the police cordon, I would risk a bullet. I realized that within a few seconds I would be led away with the others. Turning toward the bar I picked up the bartender's rag, and seizing a tray of dirty coffee cups, trotted into the kitchen.

Occasionally I would attempt to get part-time jobs. One night, employed as a handyman in a neighborhood restaurant, I noticed the proprietor sitting and talking with the last customers—three men and a woman.

There had been a short circuit downstairs; I approached the table, motioning to the proprietor. I met the woman's startled, uncertain glance and instantly exaggerated my role: I slapped my right ear several times as the men guffawed. She blushed, as if ashamed of her companions, but she continued to watch me.

The woman returned several days later accompanied by a man I had not seen before. It was late and most of the tables were empty. Since the proprietor was away, I went to the two as soon as they were seated. The woman's left hand lay palm down on the tablecloth, and she was attentively rubbing her cuticles with her right forefinger. I emptied the ashtray and adjusted the napkins and cutlery. The man asked for something, and when I shrugged meekly, the woman spoke, perhaps explaining that she had seen me before and that I could neither hear nor speak. The man scrutinized me coldly, then relaxed as I brushed an invisible speck of dust from the tablecloth. The woman nervously crumpled her handkerchief, obviously conscious of my proximity. I withdrew without turning around and again slapped my ears.

Next day I was summoned by the proprietor,

who explained in gestures that I had to do a different job. An hour later one of the waiters led me to a tall apartment house, where we took an elevator to the top floor. The door was opened by the woman I had seen in the restaurant.

I was hired to clean her apartment after the large parties she regularly gave. The parties, catered by the restaurant where I had worked, were often attended by the underworld. I was careful not to wander too close to the rooms with locked doors. I knew of too many people who had vanished from that quarter of the city because of their curiosity. After several days my presence and the hum of my vacuum cleaner went as unnoticed as the familiar creaking of the floorboards or the intermittent rattle of the steam pipes.

While dusting the furniture I covertly watched the woman's face reflected in mirrors: her image split into fragments as she rearranged her hair. I would smile politely when I caught her hesitant glance.

I worked undisturbed because my duties were simple and I needed no instruction. I noticed that when my new employer wanted to tell me something she became self-conscious and was upset by my violent ear-slappings.

Several times she tested me. Once when I was dusting, she silently approached the piano and struck a chord. Another time, as I was putting away the wine glasses, she came from behind and suddenly shouted.

I managed to restrain even the smallest twitch. One evening, without looking at me, she motioned for me to follow her.

She forgot herself completely as she stretched under me, her eyes straining toward the headboard. Her whole body became involved in drawing breath, driven by tides and currents flowing and ebbing in rapid surges. Swaying like a clump of weed in the sea, she quivered, a rushing stream of words broke over her lips like foam. It was as if I were the master of all this fluid passion, and her tumbling words its final wave.

In her last outpouring she broke into a language I could understand, and spoke of herself as a zealot entering a church built long ago from the ruins of pagan temples, a novice in the inner sanctum of the church, not knowing at whose altar she knelt, to which god she prayed.

Her voice grew rough and hoarse as she writhed on the bed, thrashing from side to side. I held her arms and shook her, diving into her with all my weight. Like a joyous mare in its solitary stall, she cried out again and again, as though trying to detach into speech what had been fused with her flesh. She whispered that she veered toward the sun, which would melt her with its heat. Her sentences poured and broke, and she muttered that the sun left only the glow of stars brushing close to each other. Slowly her lips grew parched —she slept.

•

There were rumors that a revolution was about to break out in another country. Its central government was falling apart. The country was divided into two camps: on one side the students and the farmers who opposed the President; on the other, the workers who felt the time was ripe for their party to stage a coup. The President, rumors had it, sided with the party, convinced that it would receive aid from a neighboring country where it had held power for almost two decades.

For me this was an opportunity. I had never seen or been involved in a revolution; all I had ever done was read about them or watch them on television newsreels.

I left my job and the next day was on a plane. After landing at the palm-fringed airport, I deposited my suitcase in a small hotel and mingled with the large groups of men who roamed the city. More and more of them now carried arms and banners. As I did not understand their language, I played a deaf-mute, and I played my part well.

Each group I joined claimed me as its own, handing me weapons and insignia as if convinced that it was the most natural thing in the world for a spastic to fight for the future they envisioned for their country.

Early one evening a series of explosions shook the capital. When I was ordered to a large truck loaded with assorted weapons, I knew the coup had begun. As we drove through the darkened city, our headlights outlined other armed units crossing our path and entrenching themselves behind overturned buses and makeshift barricades. Soon we saw the dead lying in pools of blood on the sidewalks, like abandoned sacks of wheat. Other bands of armed men joined us, and we raced toward the outskirts of the city. The trucks stopped and we jumped down, carrying our rifles and long knives. In a few moments we had surrounded a group of buildings. The men entered the houses; the rest of us stood expectantly in the background.

The captives were brought out one after another, many of them half naked. Not knowing what had happened, some of them tried to ask questions or say something, but were quickly silenced. Inside the buildings women screamed and children cried. The number of prisoners in front of us kept increasing, and soon there were dozens.

The commander of our group ordered the prisoners to turn and face the wall. I was certain that they were about to be shot. Not wanting to participate in the execution, I gestured to the man next to me, offering to exchange my rifle for his long knife. The man agreed. I was just about to hide behind one of the trucks when I was roughly pushed forward by men also armed with knives. Each of us was ordered to stand directly behind one of the prisoners.

I glanced around me: the armed men, tense and ready, stood at my sides and behind me. Only then did I realize that the prisoners were about to be beheaded. My refusal to obey orders would mean my being executed with those who stood in front of me. I could no longer see their faces, but their shirts were only a few inches from the blade of my knife.

It was inconceivable, I thought, that I would have to slash the neck of another man simply because events had placed me behind his back. What I was about to do was inescapable, yet so unreal that it became sense-less: I had to believe I was not myself any more and that whatever happened would be imaginary. I saw myself as someone else who felt nothing, who stood calm and composed, determined enough to stiffen his arms, to grasp and raise the weapon, to cut down the obstacle in his path. I knew I was strong enough to do it. I could recall the precision with which I had felled young trees: I could hear their moaning and creaking, and see their trembling, and I knew I could jump aside as they cracked and fell, their leaves brushing my feet.

WHEN I'M GONE, I'll be for you just another
memory descending upon you uninvited, stirring up your
thoughts, confusing your feelings. And then you'll recog-
nize yourself in this woman.

●

She looked into the room. His bed was made and the curtains were open. She turned and slowly walked downstairs.

The hall porter sat behind his desk. Embarrassed by her approach, he barely nodded. She pretended to be looking at the postcards on the swivel rack, but peered surreptitiously at the desk. On a corner of the shelf she saw several envelopes addressed by him. The porter noted her glance and picked up the letters.

"They're all marked 'registered,'" he said. "That's why they haven't been mailed yet. The boy is going to take them to the post office." He looked at her, expecting some comment. When she said nothing, he shuffled the letters, and she noticed that some were addressed to banks, others to law firms. The porter put the envelopes aside. "The gentleman departed this morning," he said. "He just left these letters, the money, and instructions. He said he wasn't coming back." He hesitated, then said: "Will you be staying on alone?"

She looked at his perspiring forehead. "I don't know," she said. "I don't know yet."

She undressed, entered the ocean, and started swimming. She felt the movement of her body and the chill of the water. A small rotten brown leaf brushed against her lips.

/ 147

Taking a deep breath, she dove beneath the surface. On the bottom a shadow glided over the seaweed, lending life and motion to the ocean floor. She looked up through the water to find its source and caught sight of the tiny leaf that had touched her before.

ABOUT THE AUTHOR

Jerzy Kosinski was born in Poland in 1933 and emigrated to the United States in 1957. He studied at the New School for Social Research and Columbia University and holds Master of Arts degrees in both history and political science. He has taught English prose and criticism at Princeton, Wesleyan and Yale and has been a Ford and Guggenheim fellow. He is a recipient of the Award in Literature of the National Institute of Arts and Letters and in 1973 was elected to serve as the president of the American Center of P.E.N. His other novels include *The Painted Bird*, which won Le Prix du Meilleur Livre Etranger in France for the best foreign work of fiction in 1965, *Being There* (1971), *Pinball* (1982), and, most recently, *The Hermit of 69th Street* (1988). *Steps* won the National Book Award in 1968. In addition, he has written literary criticism and two volumes on collective behavior, *The Future Is Ours, Comrade* (1960) and *No Third Path* (1962), which appeared under the pen name of Joseph Novak. He lives in New York City.

VINTAGE
CONTEMPORARIES

"Today's novels for the readers of today." — <u>VANITY FAIR</u>

"Real literature—originals and important reprints—in attractive, inexpensive paperbacks."—<u>THE LOS ANGELES TIMES</u>

"Prestigious."—<u>THE CHICAGO TRIBUNE</u>

"A very fine collection."—<u>THE CHRISTIAN SCIENCE MONITOR</u>

"Adventurous and worthy." — <u>SATURDAY REVIEW</u>

"If you want to know what's on the cutting edge of American fiction, then these are the books you should be reading."
 — <u>UNITED PRESS INTERNATIONAL</u>

On sale at bookstores everywhere, but if otherwise unavailable, may be ordered from us. You can use this coupon, or phone (800) 638-6460.

Please send me the Vintage Contemporaries books I have checked on the reverse. I am enclosing $ _____ (add $1.00 per copy to cover postage and handling). Send check or money order—no cash or CODs, please. Prices are subject to change without notice.

NAME _____

ADDRESS _____

CITY _____ STATE _____ ZIP _____

Send coupons to:
RANDOM HOUSE, INC., 400 Hahn Road, Westminster, MD 21157
ATTN: ORDER ENTRY DEPARTMENT
Allow at least 4 weeks for delivery.

005 38

VINTAGE
CONTEMPORARIES

___ **Love Always** by Ann Beattie	$5.95	74418-7
___ **First Love and Other Sorrows** by Harold Brodkey	$5.95	72970-6
___ **The Debut** by Anita Brookner	$5.95	72856-4
___ **Cathedral** by Raymond Carver	$4.95	71281-1
___ **Bop** by Maxine Chernoff	$5.95	75522-7
___ **Dancing Bear** by James Crumley	$5.95	72576-X
___ **One to Count Cadence** by James Crumley	$5.95	73559-5
___ **The Wrong Case** by James Crumley	$5.95	73558-7
___ **The Last Election** by Pete Davies	$6.95	74702-X
___ **A Narrow Time** by Michael Downing	$6.95	75568-5
___ **Days Between Stations** by Steve Erickson	$6.95	74685-6
___ **Rubicon Beach** by Steve Erickson	$6.95	75513-8
___ **A Fan's Notes** by Frederick Exley	$7.95	72915-3
___ **A Piece of My Heart** by Richard Ford	$5.95	72914-5
___ **The Sportswriter** by Richard Ford	$6.95	74325-3
___ **The Ultimate Good Luck** by Richard Ford	$5.95	75089-6
___ **Fat City** by Leonard Gardner	$5.95	74316-4
___ **Within Normal Limits** by Todd Grimson	$5.95	74617-1
___ **Airships** by Barry Hannah	$5.95	72913-7
___ **Dancing in the Dark** by Janet Hobhouse	$5.95	72588-3
___ **November** by Janet Hobhouse	$6.95	74665-1
___ **Fiskadoro** by Denis Johnson	$5.95	74367-9
___ **The Stars at Noon** by Denis Johnson	$5.95	75427-1
___ **Asa, as I Knew Him** by Susanna Kaysen	$4.95	74985-5
___ **A Handbook for Visitors From Outer Space** by Kathryn Kramer	$5.95	72989-7
___ **The Chosen Place, the Timeless People** by Paule Marshall	$6.95	72633-2
___ **Suttree** by Cormac McCarthy	$6.95	74145-5
___ **The Bushwhacked Piano** by Thomas McGuane	$5.95	72642-1
___ **Nobody's Angel** by Thomas McGuane	$6.95	74738-0
___ **Something to Be Desired** by Thomas McGuane	$4.95	73156-5
___ **To Skin a Cat** by Thomas McGuane	$5.95	75521-9
___ **Bright Lights, Big City** by Jay McInerney	$5.95	72641-3
___ **Ransom** by Jay McInerney	$5.95	74118-8
___ **River Dogs** by Robert Olmstead	$6.95	74684-8
___ **Norwood** by Charles Portis	$5.95	72931-5
___ **Clea & Zeus Divorce** by Emily Prager	$6.95	75591-X
___ **A Visit From the Footbinder** by Emily Prager	$6.95	75592-8
___ **Mohawk** by Richard Russo	$6.95	74409-8
___ **Anywhere But Here** by Mona Simpson	$6.95	75559-6
___ **Carnival for the Gods** by Gladys Swan	$6.95	74330-X
___ **Myra Breckinridge and Myron** by Gore Vidal	$8.95	75444-1
___ **The Car Thief** by Theodore Weesner	$6.95	74097-1
___ **Taking Care** by Joy Williams	$5.95	72912-9